A MOTHER FOR THE GP'S SON

ANNIE CLAYDON

MEDICAL ROMANCE

ISBN-13: 978-1-335-99381-6

A Mother for the GP's Son

For questions and comments about the quality of this book, please contact us at CustomerService@Harlequin.com.

Harlequin Enterprises ULC
22 Adelaide St. West, 41st Floor
Toronto, Ontario M5H 4E3, Canada
www.Harlequin.com

HarperCollins Publishers
Macken House, 39/40 Mayor Street Uppe
Dublin 1, D01 C9W8, Ireland
www.HarperCollins.com

Printed in U.S.A.

1 2 3 4 5 6 7 8 9 10 HDC 28 27 26 25

Beside the kettle was a packet of tea bags and a jar of coffee, along with a packet of chocolate biscuits.

When Alice got to her feet and walked to the fridge, it was on and contained a pint of milk. Dan must have popped in and left them on his way to the station.

She filled the kettle, switching it on, and murmured a thank-you to him. Dad had been right to trust him—he was a thoughtful and kind friend.

Who was she trying to kid? There was something about Dan's relaxed smile that told her he was the kind of man who'd take his time with a woman. Something about the controlled grace of his movements that suggested that once he had, there would be something more... Something that might take her breath away.

Seven months ago, Alice would have been open to finding out what lay beneath that lazy charm of his. But now? It was just too bad that she wasn't in the market for a nice guy with a touch of the rogue in his smile.

Dear Reader,

Sometimes we love the place we grew up in, and sometimes feelings are mixed. But I've never met anyone who is entirely indifferent to where they come from.

It's been many years since Dr. Alice Allenby has returned to the village where she was born and brought up, but the death of her father brings her back. She's determined to leave again as soon as she can, but then she meets Dr. Dan Ryan. He might just be the person to help her work through her grief, and rebuild her shattered career, but there's a catch. Alice finds herself wanting more than just a friendship with Dan, but being with him means that she must stay in the village she's vowed to leave behind forever.

Thank you for reading Alice and Dan's story. I hope that you feel as welcome in the village as I did!

Annie x

Cursed with a poor sense of direction and a propensity to read, **Annie Claydon** spent much of her childhood lost in books. A degree in English literature followed by a career in computing didn't lead directly to her perfect job—writing romance for Harlequin—but she has no regrets in taking the scenic route. She lives in London, a city where getting lost can be a joy.

Books by Annie Claydon

Harlequin Medical Romance

Jet Set Docs

The Doctor's Italian Escape

Royal York Hospital

Mistletoe Kiss to Heal His Heart

Stranded with the Island Doctor
Snowbound by Her Off-Limits GP
Cinderella in the Surgeon's Castle
Children's Doc to Heal Her Heart
One Summer in Sydney
Healed by Her Rival Doc
Country Fling with the City Surgeon
Winning Over the Off-Limits Doctor
Neurosurgeon's IVF Mix-Up Miracle
The GP's Seaside Reunion
From French Kiss to Father

Visit the Author Profile page
at Harlequin.com for more titles.

With grateful thanks to the many people
who have walked with me on the winding road
from one book to fifty.

And to Joe, Jordan and Stuart,
who have made sure that the roof above my head will
last for much longer than it takes to write another fift

CHAPTER ONE

THE TRAIN PULLED into the station. It had lost all but the front three of its carriages on the way here from London and now that it had reached the end of the line there were only a few passengers left. Clearly, not many people wanted to go to the small country villages which surrounded the station, and Dr Alice Allenby could quite agree with the sentiment. She really didn't want to be here either.

She gripped the silver-handled walking stick, cool against the palm of her hand. It felt like all she had left to lean on, now that her father was gone and the injury to her knee made it impossible to do the job she loved. For the near future at least, and who knew how long after that…

Alice climbed carefully down from the train, smilingly refusing help from a fellow passenger who offered to lift her case for her. That brittle smile, which acted as a barrier between her and a world that currently wasn't turning the way she wanted it to.

Pulling herself up to her full height, she scanned the platform. She'd only met Dr Daniel Ryan once, at her father's funeral six months ago. He'd seemed tall, and she remembered a shock of blond hair and a pair of kind blue eyes. Most of all he'd been the only person who'd asked her, instead of telling her, what she needed. Alice had been grateful for that, and for the way he'd calmly extracted her from the crowd of mourners in the church, when she'd said she wanted a little time alone to gather her thoughts before everyone made their way to the village hall for the celebration of her father's life.

Dr Ryan had kept his distance since then, leaving Alice to dictate the pace. He'd run the medical practice that her father had founded in the village, and which he and her father had latterly co-owned. But something had to be done now, and Alice had reluctantly returned to Mallory Cross to settle her father's affairs.

And now Daniel Ryan was walking—no, sauntering—towards her along the platform. Wearing a casual tan-coloured suit and a relaxed smile which no doubt concealed a thorough assessment of her gait, and a tentative diagnosis. Probably an early estimation of her strength…

Alice was strong. She was going to *have* to be, for the next couple of weeks.

'Daniel Ryan. But most people call me Dan.' He didn't take it for granted that she would remember him, although close-up he seemed unforgettable. 'Did you have a pleasant journey?'

He was talking about the train, wasn't he? Not the other journey that had led her here.

'Yes. Thanks.'

He smiled suddenly, sending an unwelcome quiver down her spine. He'd dispensed with the usual handshake, clearly understanding that it would prompt an awkward moment while she transferred her stick to her left hand. 'May I take your case?'

Okay, so he wasn't going to ask about her knee. Or not yet, anyway. And those relaxed good manners of his were difficult to resist.

'Thanks. That would be helpful.' She tipped the case onto its wheels and as Dan reached forward, catching the handle, she caught a hint of his scent.

'I'm parked right outside.'

Code for not too far to walk. Although he'd probably be noticing how well she managed the steps outside the station. Dan strolled towards the ticket office, waiting for her to negotiate the barriers before taking his platform ticket from his pocket, then led her towards a blue four-by-four which looked capable of negotiating pretty much anything that stood between him and his patients.

No doubt he was aware that someone who worked with the air ambulance service would be agile enough to get into a car, however high the chassis and despite a walking stick. And no doubt he'd be quick enough to steady her if she stumbled; she could see a spark of knowingness beneath his lazy gaze. Alice made the passenger seat unassisted and Dan closed the door. She had a few moments to settle herself while he put her case into the boot and walked round to the driving seat. Something told her that she was going to need all of her wits about her in her dealings with Dan Ryan.

The stick was new; Alice had shown no signs of having injured her leg at the funeral. From the way she walked, the problem was clearly to do with her left knee, and Dan wondered if it was a long-standing injury. The fitness requirements of her job indicated not, but the silver-handled stick wasn't a throwaway possession. He was in the midst of deciding between a broken patella and a severe dislocation by the time they reached the car. Clearly, Alice wasn't going to volunteer the information, and Dan wasn't going to ask. Not yet, anyway. Professional interest would have to wait.

Personal interest was a bit more impatient, though. Dan had noticed her blonde hair, cut short and curling gently at the nape of her neck, when he'd first met her. He hadn't noticed her eyes, which made mud-coloured seem the most enigmatic and intriguing hue in the spectrum. Nor had he noticed the shards of gold that glistened in them when she turned her face to the sunlight. Alice had clearly taken a physiotherapist's advice and was walking slowly but as naturally as possible. And there was a kind of grace about her which often came from the peak of fitness and belied any attempt to define it.

But there was something else. Alice had been slim when he'd seen her last, but she'd clearly lost weight since then and her loose sweater on a sunny day might be an attempt to hide it. She couldn't hide the dark rings under her eyes, though, or the sense that, beneath her obvious attempts at self-reliance, she was fragile.

He wasn't going to think about any of that—he couldn't. His mentor and then friend, Dr Patrick Allenby, might have foreseen his own sudden death, but more likely just been well organised. The letter he'd written to Dan, that Patrick had placed in the safe at work to be opened in the event of his death, had been quite unequivocal. Alice wouldn't stay long in the village, and he was counting on Dan to help her through the sale of the house and settlement of his estate.

That had gone without saying. Patrick had spent every other weekend with his daughter and they were clearly close, but Alice never came to the village. Something had happened here which had driven her away, and Dan's debt to Patrick could only be repaid to his daughter now.

'Do you miss him?' Alice had been sitting silently beside him as he drove, and the question made Dan jump.

'Yes, I do. Patrick gave me a job and helped me make a home here four years ago. I'm grateful to him as a mentor and as a friend.'

'He talked about you a lot. Said that your support in running the practice had given him the confidence to cut down on his own hours and work only three days a week. I know that he'd have wanted you to carry on there now.'

'It's what I want too.' Maybe that sounded a little too much like business talk, and Dan had resolved to leave that until Alice seemed ready. 'He was very proud of you. He gave my son a model of an air ambulance the Christmas before last, and told him all about what you do.'

Alice's lips twitched into a smile, and the golden rays of sunlight that ignited in her eyes seemed to fill the car. 'I should have come back more often…'

'I'm sure you know how much Patrick loved Mallory Cross, but I had the distinct impression that he couldn't have done without his weekends away. He always had a spring in his step when he left and a broader smile on his face when he returned.'

'Thanks.' Alice didn't sound entirely convinced, but perhaps she'd think about it and realise that Dan wasn't just saying things she wanted to hear. Patrick *had* loved his weekends away, and his daughter had been the apple of his eye.

She fell silent as they approached the village, and seemed almost watchful as he drove along the high street. Dan turned off, taking the road that led to Patrick's house, where Alice had told him she would be staying.

'I have to pick my son up from his childminder, and I was wondering whether you'd like to join us for lunch. I live a little further down from...' Dan still thought of it as Patrick's house, but it was Alice's now.

'From Dad's house?' She seemed to understand his hesitation. 'Yes, it would be nice to have something to eat, and to meet your son. Then I'll go back to Dad's and tackle the dust.'

'No need.' Patrick's letter had covered that, along with quite a few other things. 'I kept Mrs Franklin on.'

'If Rosie Franklin's been cleaning the place then I'll be hard put to find a speck of dust. Thanks for doing that—did the solicitor reimburse you?'

Alice clearly hadn't been keeping tabs on what Patrick's solicitor had been doing. Dan nodded as he turned into the drive leading to the childminder's home. 'Yes, he already had instructions and all I had to do was speak to Rosie. Your father was scrupulous about leaving all of his affairs in order.'

Alice chuckled. 'That doesn't surprise me. I guess being a doctor gives you a different attitude to death, when you've seen it for yourself so many times.'

Maybe… Dan had done what everyone else did when his wife had died five years ago. He'd cared for his baby son, who'd looked up at his father with his mother's dark eyes, and fallen apart in every other respect. Patrick had been the one who'd helped him put his life back together.

He stopped the car outside the house, telling Alice he wouldn't be a minute, and went to ring the doorbell. As soon as the door opened, Charlie came barrelling out, straight into his arms.

'Oof.' Dan swung Charlie into the air, holding the little boy tight against his shoulder. 'Did you have a nice time this morning?'

Charlie nodded. 'Bye, Mrs Morrison.'

'Bye-bye, Charlie.' Eve Morrison grinned at Dan. 'Same time on Monday?'

'Yes, thanks, Eve. Have a good afternoon…'

Charlie was wriggling in his arms, obviously intent on meeting their lunch guest, and when Dan turned he saw that Alice had got out of the car and was leaning against the passenger door. Dan set Charlie back on his feet and he ran to the car, stopping short a few yards away from Alice.

'My name's Charlie. What's yours?' Charlie held out his hand and Alice bent, shaking it solemnly. So far so good…

'I'm Alice. Nice to meet you, Charlie.'

'Are you coming to eat lunch with us?'

Alice nodded. 'Yes, I am.'

'My dad's a doctor. What's the matter with your leg?'

Way to go, Charlie. Perhaps his son thought that Dan's profession gave him permission to ask virtual strangers about their medical conditions. Although Dan had been wondering the same himself. He hurried towards the car, supposing that he really ought to divert Charlie's attention before Alice felt compelled to answer the question.

'Do you know the name for the bone that covers your knee?' Alice smiled, pointing to Charlie's knee.

'Mantella!'

'Very good! That's nearly right; it's your patella. Did your dad teach you that?'

Charlie nodded. 'He got it wrong; he said it was mantella.'

'Did I?' Dan asked Charlie.

'Maybe you said pantella. Alice says it's…'

'Patella.' She supplied the word, shooting a delicious smile in Dan's direction. 'I think your dad knows what it is.'

'Probably. You hurt your pa-tella?' Charlie obviously wasn't going to give up until he got an answer and since Alice clearly didn't mind giving one, Dan was interested to hear it.

'Yes, I did. I fell over and broke it into three pieces. But a surgeon mended it for me and it'll be all better soon.'

'Did it hurt?'

'We'll leave it there, shall we, Charlie. A broken patella *does* hurt, but Alice might not want us to ask about that.'

Charlie nodded, changing the subject. 'I like your walking stick.'

'Would you like to hold it for me while I get in the car?' Alice asked, opening the passenger door. Charlie nodded and she handed him her stick, before getting slowly back into the passenger seat. Then she held out her hand and Charlie gave her the stick back.

Dan picked Charlie up, tucking him under his arm, and the little boy laughed, kicking and waving in an approximation of swimming. 'Sorry. He's in an inquisitive phase…' No less inquisitive than his father, but Dan wasn't going to admit to that. 'It'll probably wear off by the time he's thirty.'

'So soon? That's a shame…' Alice reached for the car door and Dan closed it.

'Alice has been on a train this morning, and come a long way to see us. When we get home, do you think we should let her sit down and rest for a while? We can talk to her some more later.'

Charlie nodded sagely. 'Good idea, Dad…'

Charlie was as good as his word, waiting until Alice was seated comfortably on the sofa, her left leg propped on a footstool, and then running upstairs to his room. Dan busied himself in the kitchen, trying not to wonder how long it had been since Alice's surgery, and what range of knee flexion she'd achieved since then. He'd bought this house because of its modern, airy feel and the open-plan layout, which afforded him a view of the living and dining areas and allowed him to keep an eye on Charlie while he was preparing their meals. He could see Alice sitting still and quiet, apparently lost in her thoughts.

She seemed tired suddenly, as if the effort of getting here had taken its toll. When Alice thought that no one was looking, her air of fragility was more marked.

He wanted to go to her, sit down on the sofa and comfort her—about everything. Her father's death was still a raw wound, and she'd suffered a serious injury which meant she wouldn't be able to work until she was passed as fit. And something else. Whatever had kept her away from the village while Patrick was alive was clearly still worrying Alice. Perhaps more so, now that he wasn't there to help her.

Dan had been frustrated about the delays and obvious fobbing-off from Alice's solicitor over the last couple of months. Wanted to get things settled so that he could move on and look at recruiting a permanent doctor, who could never replace the enormous gap which Patrick had left but would at least bring the practice up to full strength. But he'd kept his cool, reminding himself that grief took many forms, and waited. He was glad he had now, because Alice clearly needed time to work through all the things that were making her so sad.

'Would you like to play with my helicopter?' Charlie's voice sounded from the hallway. Dan moved to usher him away, and then froze as Alice's smile lit the room.

'Yes, please!'

Charlie ran to the sofa and laid his toy helicopter onto the cushion next to Alice. Then he pulled at the comforter that lay over the back of the sofa.

'This is my own special blanket,' Charlie told her, fingering the edges of the quilt that his mother had made for him when he was born. 'It makes me better when I feel ill. Would you like to put it onto your patella?'

Dan felt his eyes fill with tears. Somehow, Charlie had sensed Alice's vulnerability and his beautiful son was trying to help her. He couldn't be more proud of him.

'This is your special thing, Charlie. Will that

be okay with your dad?' Dan had retreated to the other side of the kitchen, not daring to break the spell by watching them, but Alice must have seen Charlie's name embroidered lovingly on the quilt.

'Yes. He likes making people better.'

'Okay. Thank you.'

Dan listened as the two of them talked together, Alice telling Charlie all about the air ambulance and what it was like to fly in a helicopter. He'd been wrong when he'd thought that he might be the person to help Alice. His son seemed to be making a far better job of it.

He delayed lunch as long as he could to give Charlie and Alice some time to talk, but a lasagne could only stay in the oven for so long. When he brought it to the table, along with a salad, he saw that Charlie had placed some of his miniature action figures in awkward poses on the sofa, and that the air ambulance was working hard to collect them all up and take them to hospital.

'Dad…' Charlie ran over to him. 'I'm going to be an air ambulance pilot when I grow up. And a doctor.'

Alice laughed, taking the quilt from over her legs and folding it carefully across the back of the sofa. 'You can't be both, Charlie. The pilot flies the helicopter while the doctor looks after the people.' She turned her mouth down at Charlie's look of disappointment. 'Although you could be a doctor and fly a helicopter in your spare time. How does that sound?'

Charlie nodded his approval. 'I think I'll do that then.'

'Sounds like a plan.' Dan grinned at his son, reckoning that he could probably do anything he set his mind to. 'Go and wash your hands. You can bring your helicopter to the table if you like…'

CHAPTER TWO

ALICE HAD EATEN more in one sitting than she had for some time. Country air, perhaps. Or, more likely, the easy conversation across the dinner table. Charlie's questions about working as part of an air ambulance crew let Alice believe that anything was possible. That she'd make it back to full fitness, and the job that she loved. That this visit to Mallory Cross might not be as difficult as she'd expected. And that maybe she'd be able to make the fond farewell to her father that his funeral had failed to provide her with.

Dan cleared the table and made coffee, taking it through to the conservatory at the back of the house, while Charlie resumed the rescue of action figures from the sofa with his air ambulance.

'You like gardening?' The thriving plants around them were clearly the result of regular care.

'Yeah. I find it relaxing.' Dan looked around at the greenery. 'I often spend an hour or so in here in the evenings, winding down after Charlie goes to bed.'

'Dad told me that you're a single parent. It must be hard looking after him on your own.'

Something flickered at the side of Dan's face. Her father had never told her any more about Dan's circumstances, and perhaps she'd strayed unwittingly into a no-go area.

'My wife died when Charlie was just a baby.'

'I'm so sorry.' The familiar words that Alice had been on the receiving end of sprang to her lips. Only this time they seemed to mean something—Alice *was* sorry, for Dan and Charlie's loss. 'I didn't realise…when I allowed Charlie to put his quilt across my legs.'

Dan smiled suddenly. 'That's okay. It's one of his precious things and I'm proud that he thought it might help you too, and wanted to share it.'

'He's a really great kid. A credit to you.'

'He's a lot like his mother…'

That must hurt. 'Then he's a credit to her as well.'

'Thank you.' Dan's smile broadened. 'He is. Nola and I thought we had all the time in the world, we worked hard to build a future for ourselves. When she died, I realised that nothing could compensate for all of the time we *didn't* spend together and made a promise that I wasn't going to make the same mistake with Charlie. I decided to leave London, and from the time I first interviewed with your father I knew this was the kind of place I wanted to be. Your father saw something in me—I've never been sure what—and he was very good to me and Charlie. He gave us a new start.'

So she'd been busy running away from the village, while Dan had run to it. That was a shame. Their mutual connection with her father might have provided a basis for friendship, and Alice suspected that Dan would make a good friend. But he'd chosen to live in the one place in the world that she didn't want to spend too much time in.

'Dad thought a great deal of you, too. He told me that you were the best doctor he'd ever met and that he was lucky to have you in the practice.'

Dan chuckled. 'He must have meant second-best. His daughter was the best.'

This was nice. Two people who'd cared about her father and known him well, finding a connection in their mutual regard for him. If she'd stayed a little longer at the funeral, spent more time talking with Dan, then maybe Alice would have found the closure she needed sooner.

'I was wondering…' Dan's voice broke her reverie. 'You know how your father always loved the garden around the surgery…'

'Yes. He reckoned that in the summer the garden did his patients as much good as he did. He put a few benches out there under the trees and people used to congregate there.'

Dan nodded. 'Several of those trees died a couple of years ago, and he never got around to replanting them. I was wondering if you would give your blessing for me to do that now, along with a new garden seat, in his memory.'

This feeling of solace, stealing over her like a warm comforter, was what Alice had been searching for. 'On one condition.'

'Name it.'

'That you allow me to add a tree or two of my own. And help you plant them.'

'That would be my privilege.' Dan's blue eyes rippled with the kind of warmth that reminded her of a sun-kissed ocean. 'We could choose some trees and a suitable bench together if you'd like?'

'Thank you. Yes, let's set aside a day.' Leaving a memorial to her father behind, in the place that he'd loved, was something that Alice could commit herself to. Why hadn't she thought of this herself?

Dan leaned back in his seat. 'It might have to be two half days. Or four quarters… Things have been busy for the practice.'

He was looking remarkably relaxed about it, but maybe that was his way of dealing with panic.

'My solicitor said there was a note of urgency in your letter to him. How bad are things here?'

'We're managing. We had a temporary doctor here, Dr Ramesh Singh, and he was excellent. But he wanted a permanent job back in London, that's where his girlfriend lives. He got a really good offer and left us three weeks ago. His replacement, Dr Greene, has been here for two and a half weeks and although he's a good doctor he's made it clear that he's not reckoning on this being a permanent job. It's not an ideal situation for us, in terms of continuity for our patients, but young doctors see the city as providing more opportunity.'

His tone assumed that Alice had the same priorities. Maybe she did, but that wasn't why she hadn't come back. At one point she'd supposed that she'd be joining her father's practice when she'd completed her GP training, but then events had overtaken her.

'Dad knew that I wasn't interested in working here at the practice. That's why he divided up his half share as he did—five percent to you and forty-five to me. When he wrote his will he discussed it with me and told me that it would give you a fifty-five percent controlling share, and me the cash from the rest.'

Dan nodded. 'That was very fair of him. I'd be willing to sign that five percent over to you if you wanted…'

'I don't want it!' Alice realised she'd snapped at him. 'Sorry. It's a generous offer but coming back here isn't anywhere on my list of things to do next. You've put in a lot of work here, and Dad knew that it would be best for the practice and its future if you were in control. I'd like to sell my part of it, either to you or to someone nominated by you, if you're open to that.'

'We'd have to get an independent valuation and agree a sum, but subject to that I'd like to make you an offer.' Dan was watching her intently, waiting for her reaction, and Alice smiled.

'That would be my first choice. I'll be here for at least another week, to get a start on sorting the house out, so there's time for us to work out the details.'

He nodded, smiling that lazy smile that made Alice feel that anything was possible. 'Thanks. If you're planning on being here for that long, then perhaps Charlie and I could take you over to the supermarket? My fridge could do with stocking up as well.'

'Could you give me a lift over to the house, and drop me there? I have a food delivery coming at four.'

'Sure.' Dan didn't move. 'There's plenty of time, we'll finish our coffee first.'

The supermarket suddenly felt like a much less challenging place to visit than her old home. When they drew up outside her father's house, the two-hundred-year-old property with its country garden hadn't changed. Neat and carefully tended, as if Dad was about to appear at the front door.

'You've arranged for a gardener to come in?' Alice swallowed down the lump that had formed in her throat.

'We took care of your garden!' Charlie exclaimed gleefully from the child seat behind her and Alice turned.

'You did? Did your dad help?'

'Dad mowed the lawn. I pulled up all the weeds.'

'And hardly any of the plants…' Dan murmured and Charlie ignored him.

'Thank you, Charlie. You've done a wonderful job; the garden looks lovely. Just as I remember it.' Alice concealed her tears by leaning forward to get out of the car, and Dan hurried to the back seat to unbuckle Charlie's seatbelt.

'We'll help Alice with her bag, eh, Charlie?' Dan seemed to be taking a long time over getting her case from the boot, leaving Alice to walk up the front path alone. As she reached the clematis vine that grew around the porch, she could even smell the familiar vanilla scent of coming home.

Alice fumbled with her set of keys, turning as she got the front door open to find that Dan had quite needlessly stopped halfway up the front path to point something out to Charlie. When he saw her waiting for him, he shepherded Charlie towards the porch.

He leaned through the open doorway, putting her case in the hall. 'Is there anything we can do for you?'

In other words, did she want to be alone or could she do with some company? Having Dan's quiet support and Charlie's happy chatter seemed suddenly necessary in facing the empty rooms ahead of her. That was why she needed to do this alone.

'No. Thanks, but I'd like some time to myself.'

Dan nodded. 'You have my number. If I don't hear from you, perhaps we'll speak tomorrow?'

In other words, there are no rules. When something seems too hard, you get to ask for whatever you need.

'Thanks. Are you working tomorrow?'

'I'm on call—Dr Greene's agreed to cover the surgery. We have an agreement with three other practices to each cover one Saturday in four and it's our turn tomorrow.'

'What's the best time to call you?'

Dan grinned. 'Any time. Surprise me.'

He took Charlie's hand and the boy said his goodbyes. Alice waited for them to get into the car, and waved as it drew away. Then she stepped into the hallway, and shut the door behind her.

The silence came crashing down on her, leaving Alice with just her thoughts and the noise of memories echoing from every room. On autopilot, she walked through to the kitchen, sitting down at the table. A cup of tea would be nice, she should have thought of that sooner…

Beside the kettle was a packet of teabags and a jar of coffee, along with a packet of chocolate biscuits. When she got to her feet and walked to the fridge, it was on and contained a pint of milk. Dan must have popped in and left them here for her.

She filled the kettle, switching it on, and murmured a *thank-you* to him. Dad had been right to trust him; he was a thoughtful and kind friend.

Who was she trying to kid? There was something about Dan's relaxed smile that told her he was the kind of man who'd take his time with a woman. Something about the controlled grace of his movements which suggested that once he had there would be something more… Something that might take her breath away.

Six months ago, Alice would have been open to finding out what lay beneath that lazy charm of his. But now? It was just too bad that she wasn't in the market for a nice guy with a touch of roguishness in his smile.

CHAPTER THREE

SERIOUSLY? OF ALL the days for Tom Greene to wake up with a fever and flu symptoms. Eve Morrison had been unable to look after Charlie for a few hours and Dan had ended up bringing him into the surgery and asking the receptionist to keep an eye on him. The practice nurse was here, working her way through an ever-growing number of children who required vaccinations, and there was a full list of patients for Dan to see.

And then Alice called. She sounded rested and rather more cheerful than she had yesterday. 'Now that I have my shopping, I can offer you and Charlie lunch.'

'I'd love to but I can't make it…' As Dan recounted the list of reasons he felt sharp regret pierce his heart.

'I'll be there in half an hour.' This resolve in Alice's voice was new, and Dan couldn't help liking it. A lot.

'There's no need—we'll manage. But…thanks.'

‘Am I still on the list of approved doctors for the practice?’

‘Yes, your father never removed you.’ Patrick had always known that Alice wouldn’t return, but it was a nod to his daughter. Something that reminded them both that she always had a place, here. ‘But…’

‘I can be very adaptable in an emergency.’ Alice almost seemed to be relishing the situation. ‘Even if I only make the tea then that’s something, isn’t it? See you soon.’

‘There’s no…’ Too late. Alice had already ended the call.

Dan smiled for the first time this morning.

Forty minutes later, just as he was calling up the details of his next patient on the computer system, a knock sounded at his consulting room door. Dan called for whoever it was to come in and Charlie ran into the room, beckoning to Alice to follow him. She was still walking slowly, using her stick, but in her other hand was a cup of tea, which at the moment was very welcome.

‘We’re the helicopter rescue team!’ Charlie rushed around his desk, taking an energy bar from his pocket and hugging Dan’s legs. ‘Eat this.’

‘Thanks, Charlie, that’s great. Just what I needed.’ Dan lifted his son up onto his lap and managed to give him a hug before the boy wriggled back down again and ran to Alice.

'We have things to do, don't we, Charlie?' Alice put the cup of tea down on Dan's desk and smiled down at Charlie.

'Yes. We. Do.'

Dan was suddenly in no mood to ask. The shards of gold in Alice's eyes seemed to have been recharged overnight, and were gleaming brightly. They were all that he could see, outshining the dark rings under her eyes and her gaunt frame. There was a light about her that made him want to hold her…

'Right then. We'll let you get on with your list, and we'll worry about everything else.' Alice gave him another intoxicating smile and made for the door with Charlie in tow. Suddenly the weight of the morning seemed to lift from Dan's shoulders.

When Dan heard voices outside and looked out of the window, he saw that Alice had moved the kids coming for their vaccinations out into the garden at the back of the surgery. Babies and toddlers were with their mothers on rugs spread on the lawn and the older ones were playing while they waited for their names to be called. Some of the toys from the waiting room were in evidence and there was a carefree, sunny-day atmosphere, rather than one of mums trying to keep their children quiet in the full waiting room.

On further investigation, between patients, he found that the practice nurse had lost the slightly harassed look of earlier this morning and was relaxed and smiling—getting through her work much more quickly as a consequence. He saw Alice sitting with Molly, the receptionist, looking through the list of patients, and it was obvious from the order of people he was seeing that a little informal triage work was going on.

Simple, easy things that made such a difference. If he hadn't been so rushed this morning he would have done exactly what Alice was doing, and Dan saw Patrick's hand in all of this. He'd always tried to make the surgery a happy place where patients could feel at home, and that ethic had clearly rubbed off on his daughter.

But she was making it her own. Bringing the light of her smile and those extraordinary eyes to the situation, and helping everyone to get on with their work in the understaffed, over-stretched surgery.

By one o'clock they were done, which was something of an achievement on everyone's part. Molly had offered to take Charlie home to give him some lunch and then she and her husband, who was a model train enthusiast, would take him to see an exhibition that was being held at one of the local town halls. Dan had given in to Charlie's imploring eyes, thanked Molly and turned his attention to the visits he needed to make this afternoon.

'It takes a village, doesn't it.' He smiled at Alice, who was suddenly motionless, sitting in the corner of the reception area.

'To bring up a child? Yes, sometimes it does. Dad must have told you that my mother died when I was ten.'

Dan nodded. 'Yes, he did. I'd said on my job application that I was a widower with a baby, just to make my own position clear. We spoke about it when we first met, and his advice and support meant a great deal to me. It must have been hard for you, losing your mother.'

She smiled. 'Dad's advice and support meant a lot to me, too. I wasn't as young as Charlie, but I spent a lot of time in other people's houses while Dad was working. It's a good feeling, knowing that you can just open your front door and always find someone who's a stand-in aunt or uncle. A good way for Charlie to grow up.'

So that wasn't Alice's problem with the village. Patrick had hinted that village life wasn't for everyone, and told Dan that he should know that if he was considering putting down roots here. At the time, he'd felt that Nola was the only woman he'd ever want, and meeting someone new was irrelevant.

But somewhere along the way he'd healed. Dan

hadn't noticed that until he'd seen Alice smile, and felt the once-familiar tingle run down his spine. And it was time to take Patrick's advice, because Dan and Charlie's home was here, now, and Alice's clearly wasn't.

'I think so. He's happy here and so am I.' Dan wondered whether he'd mentioned that to make his own position clear to Alice. A myriad of possibilities of *what-might-happen-next* had crossed his mind in the last twenty-four hours, and perhaps he just needed to shut them down before he was tempted to try to explore any of them.

'That's good. When life here suits you it's a great place to be.' The light in her eyes resembled golden daggers for a moment. She knew, and Alice was telling him to keep his distance.

'Let me drop you home. I have a couple of visits to make. Mrs Richardson wants to have a chat about something, and I told her not to come to the surgery this morning and that I'd go and see her when I was finished here. Then I'll pop in and see how Tom Greene is doing; he said that he thought it was just a twenty-four-hour flu but he didn't sound at all well on the phone this morning.'

'Mrs Helen Richardson? She was my teacher at school.' Alice pressed her lips together. 'If you'll give me a lift to where Dr Greene is staying, I can drop in to make sure he's okay while you go and see Helen.'

'You don't need to do that…'

'It's okay. I've missed being useful, and it's nice to be back doing something, even if I'm not fit to go back to my real job yet. If you have a spare medical bag that I can use…?'

Maybe Alice *did* need to do this. And Dan owed it to Patrick to put aside his own feelings and give Alice everything she might either want or need. Although Alice's rosy picture of a village helping to bring up a child clearly didn't include Helen Richardson.

'You can take mine. Helen just wants to discuss the results of some recent tests. I'll take you to lunch somewhere afterwards if you can spare the time?'

Alice smiled. 'I've had nothing *but* time for the last few months. Something to do that doesn't involve missing Dad, or wishing I was fit to do my job, would be very welcome.'

Dan had dropped Alice off at the small holiday rental cottage where Tom was staying and offered to come inside to introduce her, as an excuse for carrying the heavy medical bag. She'd glared at him and told him she was perfectly capable of managing on her own, and he'd had to content himself with watching her up the front path as the wheeled medical bag bumped across the paving stones. The morning's activities didn't seem to have changed her gait, and Dan wondered in passing whether the stick was partly a prop to a wounded heart in addition to being a support for an injured knee. He dismissed the thought as one to explore later.

Alice had promised to text him if she needed anything or when she'd finished with Tom, and he took his time going through Helen's recent cardiac tests with her over a cup of tea. Finally, he drove back to Tom's cottage, wondering what was taking Alice so long.

She answered the door, wearing surgical gloves and a mask, and motioned him away into the paved area in front of the house. 'Just a precaution.' Dan saw the smile in her eyes, clearly signifying that everything was under control. 'I'm not sure. Tom may have a nasty dose of the flu, but I haven't heard of any cases this summer. The mask is just a precaution; I suspect that he may have malaria.'

'What? I haven't heard that Mallory Cross's a malaria zone…' Surprise made Dan a little dismissive of the idea and he saw Alice purse her lips.

'No, but I assume you know that he was just back from holiday when he came here. In Indonesia. And before you say that the tourist areas in Indonesia have malaria-free status, I asked if I could see his phone and his social media says that he went off-piste to the Papua region for a couple of days. He had a wonderful time, apparently.'

'And it just takes one insect bite.' Dan thought for a moment. 'The incubation period for malaria isn't usually this long, but that isn't set in stone.'

Alice nodded. 'It could be something else, maybe avian flu. I gather there are warning notices around the mill pond this year. But that would be very unusual, and I'm rather hoping it's not, since it can be transmitted from person to person. And Tom's a doctor…'

'Yeah. How is he?'

'He's not at all well. I've called the hospital and explained the situation, and they're sending patient transport to take him in for tests. If it is malaria they'll need to start treatment straight away and inform the relevant authorities, since it's a notifiable disease.'

Dan nodded. 'Would you like me to go and take a look at him?'

'No, what I want you to do is to stay out here. The practice is one doctor down already and the last thing anyone needs is for you to catch something.'

It made sense. Dan didn't like it, and if Alice was right, and Tom did have malaria, there was no risk of transmitting the disease. She'd done everything right so far and he was inclined to trust her diagnosis, but the risk was one he didn't need to take.

'Okay. I'll cool my heels out here, shall I, while

you go back inside to deal with my patient.' He turned the corners of his mouth down.

'Yep. Sorry about that. It's a tough job but someone's got to do it.'

Ten minutes later the transport ambulance arrived, and after a short wait the two-person crew appeared in the doorway with Tom in a wheelchair. From his vantage point, Dan could see that he was clearly running a fever and he seemed drowsy, although he held up his hand to acknowledge Dan.

Dan gave Tom a wave back and watched as he was wheeled into the vehicle and the crew prepared for departure. Then Alice appeared in the doorway.

'He wanted me to apologise to you…' Alice shook her head. 'I told him that he has nothing to apologise for, and that he did the right thing in not coming to the surgery this morning. He should stop worrying and concentrate on getting better.'

'Thanks. I couldn't have put it better myself.'

'They're putting a rush on the tests as Tom has been in contact with patients, and we should hear back within a couple of hours.'

Dan nodded. 'He doesn't seem too bad from a distance.' Alice's decision to keep him away from Tom was absolutely in line with procedure, but it still chafed a little.

'I told you that staying away from him was the hardest thing…'

'So you did. I followed your instructions with manful resolve.'

Alice laughed suddenly. 'I noticed. Nice job.'

'Can I take you to lunch now? We can't do anything else until we hear the results of the tests. Then we may have to start worrying about whether Tom's passed anything on to our patients.' Dan realised he'd fallen into the mistake of assuming that this was Alice's problem. It really wasn't, but he almost wished that it was; her assessment of the situation had already given them a valuable head start.

'We'll cross that bridge if we come to it.' Clearly, Alice felt that she was involved now, too. 'I'm going to walk back to the house and take a shower, and you can pick me up in an hour.'

Dan raised an eyebrow. 'Isn't that taking things a bit too far?'

'Very probably. But in the circumstances, I'd be a lot happier doing that. There's a footpath that runs from here back to the house which cuts off half the distance and I'll probably be home before you are. My leg's fine.'

The resolve in Alice's face made kidnapping her out of the question.

'You're sure?'

'I'm my father's daughter. Did you ever see him not sticking to a decision?'

'No, I can't say that I did. Patrick always made good decisions, though…' Fighting with Alice was suddenly the most delicious part of the day.

She laughed. 'There you go, then. So do I.' Alice turned, making for a level track which ran along the back of the cottages, which Dan hadn't taken much notice of before. It probably would be the quickest route. If there wasn't a line of trees in the way it would be possible to see Patrick's house from here. And if her leg *was* hurting her, Alice was making a fine job of concealing it.

'See you in an hour,' he called after Alice, and she raised her hand in acknowledgement, her gaze firmly fixed on what was ahead of her.

Determined that Alice wasn't going to out-precaution him, Dan had showered and thrown his clothes into the washing machine and after spending five minutes instead of thirty seconds choosing a shirt to wear was in the car in slightly less than an hour. Alice answered the door with her hair still wet and wearing a pair of figure-hugging jeans with a bright red top.

'You're faster than I am.' She chuckled when she saw his almost-dry hair and walked into the kitchen, picking up a pair of low-heeled ankle boots on the way.

'How's the mantella?'

'Fine.' He saw Alice's knuckles whiten around the silver handle of her stick. She seemed to be walking without pain, and maybe it was the wounded heart that was bothering her. 'I've been thinking…'

'Should I worry?' Dan joined her at the kitchen table while she leaned down to put on her boots.

'I shouldn't imagine so. You're going to be busy over the next few weeks, dealing with everything on your own. My fitness-for-work assessment isn't for another month, and there's nothing I need to be home for until then. If I can square it with my boss, then perhaps I could help you out.'

Another month. Getting to know Alice, maybe finding out what made her tick. Working towards a friendship, because anything else between them would be impossible.

'I won't say that I couldn't use some help. But…' Dan wondered how to phrase his reservations.

'I don't need you to pay me, I'm on sick leave from the air ambulance service. My entitlement's gone down to half pay now, but I can manage on that. And the practice means something to me as well.'

'Granted. Only you're an equal partner in the practice and Patrick's daughter. Not paying you isn't an option for me.'

'The air ambulance service is a charity, so I'll just donate whatever you pay me back to them. Or you could do it, we can sort that out later.' Alice twisted her mouth in a sure sign that she intended to catch him in a moment of weakness and have her own way on the matter. 'And I'd expect you to take a look at my CV and interview me. Perhaps I could take a step back from the patients in the village, as you're the one who knows them best now. I could concentrate on admin and maybe taking on some of the newer patients.'

That was what was bothering him. Alice was clearly intent on helping, and not asking for any payment would give her carte blanche to pick and choose her patients carefully. That was okay, but Dan needed to know what the score was.

'This is not just curiosity on my part; it's for the sake of good working practice. Patrick never told me why you left the village and I didn't ask. But you're obviously uneasy about being here, and if we're going to be working together I need to know why.'

Alice didn't meet his gaze, which only strengthened Dan's resolve. Something bad had happened and he really did need to know what it was if he was to run the practice as efficiently as possible while taking care of everyone who worked there.

'I… Perhaps we could talk about that later?'

'Of course. Whenever you like. In the meantime, there's a new place just opened up near Silverton and I hear that they do really good burgers…' Silverton had the advantage of being twenty miles away from Mallory Cross.

'Don't you have to pick Charlie up?' Alice was clearly grabbing at straws.

'No, Molly's husband will be very disappointed if they don't get to try out as many model railways as they have time for. I gave her a call on the way here and Charlie's having a whale of a time.'

Alice nodded. 'All right. Burgers and chips do sound good at the moment, I'm really hungry. Do they do good chips?'

'I'm told they're triple-cooked.'

'In that case...' she smiled suddenly '...the place sounds unmissable.'

CHAPTER FOUR

ALICE TOOK ADVANTAGE of the drive to Silverton to think a little. And got precisely nowhere.

She'd known that sooner or later she'd probably have to mention that she didn't intend to renew her acquaintance with the village any more than necessary, but she hadn't counted on caring what Dan thought of that. What he might think of *her* when she told him why. But he was right—if she was going to work at the surgery she did need to explain her limits, if only to allow him to manage staff allocation more efficiently.

As they got out of the car Alice's phone buzzed. She pulled it from her pocket. 'That was quick. They've done the test and confirmed that Tom has malaria.' She turned the corners of her mouth down.

'It's a difficult diagnosis to make, and you made it quickly, so Tom has a good chance of a full recovery. *And* there's no chance of an epidemic going around the village…'

Dan had slipped back into relaxed mode now

and seemed at one with the pools of sunshine and greenery that surrounded the tables set out in the large open-air dining space at the back of the restaurant. As if he'd had a Saturday morning lie-in and the unwinding process of a sunny weekend was going well. The air ambulance crew knew a little something about unwinding between flights, but it seemed that Dan could teach even them a thing or two.

They dined on Wagyu beefburgers with triple-cooked chips and a side salad. In the warmth of the day, with the low hum of conversation and laughter around them, it seemed that the moment for talking might never come, but it had only been postponed.

'Coffee?' Dan asked as the waitress appeared to clear the table.

'Yes, that would be nice. We can talk…' Now that Alice had said it, there was no going back. And a flicker at one side of Dan's eye told her that he knew what they'd be talking about.

He turned to the waitress, smiling. 'Two *large* coffees, please.'

Dan was waiting. He'd put sugar and milk into his coffee, stirred it and then taken a sip. Then he leaned back in his seat, as if to enjoy the sunshine.

'Would you stop, please?' It was nice of him

to give her a little space, but his studied indifference was making her nervous.

He grinned, leaning forward to put his forearms on the table. 'Thanks. The moment was getting a little…'

'Long and awkward?'

'Yes. So, are you just going to tell me? Why you're avoiding Mallory Cross?' He moved a little closer. 'We're far enough away now, and I've been keeping an eye out to see whether we've been followed.'

Alice couldn't help smiling. Maybe she could keep her cool and deal with this after all. 'Okay. So, I was only nineteen. And I had this boyfriend…'

'Name?'

'Pete Shoesmith. Why?'

'I'm constructing a mental picture…'

Was he flirting? Alice looked into his face and saw only warm concern.

'The Shoesmiths aren't living in the village anymore, they left a while ago.' Dan gave a small nod. 'Pete and I had been going out together since sixth-form college, and I'd gone to medical school in Newcastle while Pete went to university in Exeter. We were reckoning on getting engaged when we'd finished our degrees.'

'So it was serious?'

'Maybe not as much as I thought. I used to visit him in Exeter and he came up to Newcastle, and of course we had the holidays together. But… I'd found what I wanted to do with my life and I was full of hopes and excitement for the future. Pete seemed a bit less committed to his studies. The summer at the end of that first year apart seemed as if it might turn out to be make or break for our relationship.'

'Long-distance relationships aren't easy.' Dan turned the corners of his mouth down.

'This one wasn't. I felt that I was losing touch with him. As things turned out, I was right…' Alice let out a sigh. She had to stop thinking about the best way to say this, because there was no good way.

'We'd been to the pictures together. Pete was driving and he was going really fast along the narrow roads that lead to the village. I told him to slow down but he just laughed and told me I should live a little. They were the last words he said to me, that I should live a little, because he lost control of the car and it spun off the road and went sidelong into a tree. I remembered to call the emergency services first, then I called Dad and he said he was coming out to find us.' Alice felt her eyes fill with tears.

Dan reached across the table, his fingertips just inches from hers. A little comfort would be natural at this point but that wasn't what Alice needed. Her tears were the same tears she'd cried then, in the passenger seat of the car. She'd known enough to realise that Pete was gone, and when she'd seen the headlights coming towards her from the village she'd known that her dad was on his way. It was then that she'd allowed herself to cry.

'Dad got me out of the car… I just had a few cuts and bruises. But Pete's seatbelt had come loose… Maybe he unclipped it himself, I don't know. Dad examined him and when he got back out of the car and started to walk me away, I knew that he was dead.'

'I'm sorry you had to go through that.'

'It was…' Alice had been numb with shock, relying on her dad to do all the right things. 'We waited for the ambulance to come and then Dad told the police that they could speak to me at home. He took a blood test and gave it to them…'

'But why? You were a passenger.'

'The car had gone some way off the road and from what he saw he suspected that the accident wasn't just an error in judgement on Pete's part. He asked me if I'd taken anything or been drinking and I told him no, and…he wanted to clear me of any involvement.'

Dan looked at her, clearly perplexed. Alice was going to have to say it.

'The autopsy showed that Pete had a cocktail of different drugs in his system. My blood test came back clear.'

Dan nodded. 'So he was driving under the influence of drugs but you had no part in that.'

'I didn't even know. I thought he'd changed but… I put that down to the time we'd spent away from each other. I suppose I would have realised sooner or later.'

'Assuming you survived the accident. It sounds as if you were very lucky not to have been badly hurt.'

'That was what I thought.' Alice turned the corners of her mouth down. She'd survived the accident, survived Pete's death. The next part was what she couldn't forget.

'What do you mean?'

'Pete's parents blamed me. Said I must have known about his drug-taking, and even that I'd probably supplied him with the drugs, since I was a medical student.'

Dan shook his head. 'Since when did first year medical students have greater access to drugs than any other student? They'd just lost their son and people say things they don't mean when they're faced with that kind of grief. But you must know that sounds a little crazy.'

'Yes, of course I do.' She frowned at him. 'But you know what living in a village is like. Rumours fly around before anyone's had a chance to set things straight. Dad did his best, and he stood up for me. At the coroner's inquest I was completely exonerated, but…'

'But what? Please tell me.' Dan knew they'd

reached the heart of the matter, and Alice could practically feel the warmth radiating from his eyes.

'These were people I'd grown up with. A lot of them had known me since I was a baby. I'd hoped that they might have trusted me, or given me the benefit of the doubt, but…they waited for six months, until the inquest, to accept that I wasn't to blame and some wouldn't accept it even then. That's why I haven't gone back to the village since and I'm not contemplating staying now. Because I thought I was safe there, and that I was trusted, and then it all disappeared in a second.'

'Did the young man's parents ever retract what they'd said?' Dan's face was grave now.

'I don't know. They moved away from the village, and after that summer I never went back. Dad understood why I couldn't, and I understood why he stayed. We didn't let that get in the way of our relationship.'

Dan thought for a moment. 'And an air ambulance crew… I've heard that they can be a pretty tight bunch.'

He'd worked that one out quickly.

Alice smiled. 'You heard right. I've put my life in their hands more than once, and had them do the same for me. We rely on teamwork to do what we do, and we trust each other.'

She'd told him everything now. It was too soon to ask Dan to make a decision about her working with the practice, but Alice was holding her breath. Wanting him to make a decision about *her.*

'You were strong. To get past that and use it to make something positive in your career. Patrick was rightly proud of your achievements, and I know what his advice would be now. We'd be honoured to have you join the practice for however long you feel you can give us, and I'll personally make sure that you're happy with everything that's asked of you.'

'What? You don't want to think about it? Overnight, perhaps?'

Dan leaned back in his seat, taking a sip of his coffee. 'No. If it makes any difference I could pretend to and give you a ring in the morning.'

Alice shook her head. 'You said that this was what my father's advice would be…' Was Dan doing this out of loyalty to her father?

'If you think I'm doing this just because you're Patrick's daughter then you couldn't be more wrong. His advice would be that every decision I make about the practice has to be for the good of my patients. That's why I'm accepting your offer.'

How did this guy always manage to say the right thing?

Alice held out her hand. 'Okay. It's a deal.' There was a measure of trust involved in the arrangement, but Dan had trusted her by accepting her reasons for leaving the village without question. Alice hadn't expected the word *trust* to feature heavily in her dealings here, but somehow it had crept in.

He took her hand, his fingers gentle. And there was something else, a shared warmth that seemed to permeate all of their dealings. It was the kind of warmth that Alice could lose herself in if she wasn't very careful. She tightened her grip and gave his hand a firm shake, withdrawing it quickly to rest it on the cool handle of her stick.

He felt it too, she knew he did. That moment of understanding that reached past today and into a tomorrow that wasn't going to happen. Dan shook his head, as if escaping his own thoughts about elusive tomorrows.

'Where did you find the stick? It's not standard NHS issue...'

'It belonged to Dad.' Alice bit her lip, wondering whether she should have admitted that, but it was too late now. 'He broke his ankle, years ago, and needed it for a while. He said that if he was going to have to use a stick he might as well do it in style and went up to London to one of those old-fashioned shops who do this kind of thing. It was in the umbrella stand in the hall, and when my solicitor sent someone to do an inventory of the house I asked him to fetch it for me. I had to have it cut down, but the handle's much more comfortable.'

Dan nodded. 'Good idea. Something of Patrick's to lean on.'

He didn't miss a thing, however small and insignificant. Or, in this case, however important and comforting. But there was no judgement in Dan's eyes.

'Yes.' Alice reached for her coffee, finding that it was cold. 'Do you fancy a refill? Or do you have to get back?'

'No.' Dan's grin was pure, switched-off sunny Saturday afternoon. 'It's nice here, let's stay for a while.'

It had been a long day, but there was still work to be done. Dan had settled Charlie down to sleep and then called the hospital to check on Tom. His malaria was still at the uncomplicated stage, and the prognosis was optimistic. He texted the good news through to Alice then spent some time going through the patient lists. Alice's reservations about the village didn't centre around who'd said what to whom—they were all about trust. A trust that had been broken when her boyfriend's car had ploughed into a tree.

He divided the practice's patients into long-term inhabitants of the village—the people that Alice had grown up with—and 'newcomers', which included people who'd been here for the last ten years. It was an arbitrary choice, because Dan was sure that several people on the 'long-term' list would have readily accepted that Alice wasn't at any fault, but it was the only yardstick he had.

Was this really necessary? Dan didn't think about that because it was necessary to Alice. And putting her first seemed the most natural thing in the world when she walked into his consulting room at eight o'clock on Monday morning.

A spring in her step was a little too much to ask, but there was a golden fire in her eyes. She looked every inch the doctor in a pair of dark trousers and a neat pale blue and white pinstriped blouse. And every inch a woman, her hair curling around her ears and the nape of her neck with more abandon than he'd seen before. Her fingers firm and yet somehow sensual on the silver handle of her stick.

'What's that?' He nodded towards the bag she carried, forgetting to say good morning. Maybe because, in his thoughts, Alice had never really left his side.

'Just a few bits and pieces. I called the air ambulance team when I got home on Saturday, and they opened my locker and sent everything up by overnight courier. I also contacted the operations manager, and she said it was okay for me to fill in here while I'm off sick. She's emailed me to that effect, and she'll be sending an official confirmation through to us both when she gets into work this morning.'

'Right, then.' Dan crossed the first two entries off his list of things to do. 'We're pretty well stocked with anything you might need…'

That wasn't really the point and Alice shook her head, laughing. 'So is an air ambulance. That doesn't stop us from going out with a few extras in our pockets which come in useful.'

That probably included the top-of-the-range stethoscope, engraved on the inside of the bell and sporting a cherry-red acoustic tube to match her uniform. Patrick had shown it to Dan before giving it to Alice for Christmas two years ago, and he imagined that no other stethoscope would do. Dan turned his attention to the next item on his list.

'I've made a list of several patients who have appointments later on today, and another of patients who require ongoing monitoring. Do you feel able to take them on?'

Alice shot him a glance which indicated that she felt able to take almost anything on, and scanned the lists. 'I don't recognise any of the names here.'

'You've been gone a while. People come and go.'

'Clearly.' Alice knew what he'd done, and that he'd carefully separated the people she didn't know from ones that she did. If that wasn't necessary then so be it, but she didn't seem upset about it. 'So where do I start?'

'The surgery opens at nine, which I expect you already know. So there's time to get yourself settled and take a quick look through the notes of the patients you're going to be seeing. If you have any questions, you know where I am. Which of the two spare consulting rooms would you like to set up shop in?'

In other words, did she want to take her father's consulting room or the smaller one that the temporary doctors had been using? Alice met his gaze. 'I'm a little surprised that you haven't moved into the larger one. As you're now head of the practice.'

'We gathered up all of Patrick's personal things from there, and took them to the house. The boxes are in—'

'I saw them.' A shadow fell across Alice's face. 'I haven't had a chance to go through them yet.'

That was fine, she'd do it when she was ready. 'I like this one. I know where everything is.' And if Alice was going to work here, even for just a few weeks, then he'd prefer she had the choice of the other two.

'Okay. I'll take Dad's consulting room if that's all right? Since I know where everything is.'

'That's great.' Dan got to his feet, wishing that he'd been a little less businesslike and a lot more personal. That he'd at least acknowledged the insistent bond he felt with her. 'You've seen the new coffee machine?'

'I did notice it the other day, but never got a chance to try it out.' Alice grinned at him in a very un-businesslike way, which made his heart lurch suddenly.

'Right, then.' Dan found that he was smiling back. 'Molly's committed to trying all of the different flavours, and there are a few that I'd advise you to avoid…'

CHAPTER FIVE

ALICE SANK INTO her father's chair, wondering if maybe the smaller consulting room might not have been the better choice. But adjusting the height and tilt of the seat made her feel a little less like a kid sitting in Dad's chair.

Sunshine was streaming in through the French windows that looked out onto the garden. It was different now, the trees were larger than she remembered them and the bushes around the perimeter had grown together into a well clipped hedge.

She could smell the scent of hazelnut-flavoured coffee from the cup that Dan had carried in for her and put onto the desk. One of Molly's experimental flavours that Dad would have found too sweet, and from the look on his face Dan didn't think much of either. And when she switched on the computer, typing in her name and the password Dan had given her, this felt a little more like somewhere she ought to be. Alice took her stethoscope from her bag, finding a place for it on the desk, and then the picture of her in her air ambulance uniform, hugging her father, which had been in one of the carefully packed boxes from the surgery which she'd found in the spare room yesterday.

He was still here. But Alice had to fill the seat behind the desk now, while Dad smiled at her from the photograph. Alice picked up the lists that Dan had made, which seemed now like a first step on a new way forward, and started work.

'How are you doing?' Dan knocked on the door and sauntered into her office at two o'clock, shortly after Alice had heard his last patient leave. She'd already eaten most of the sandwiches that Molly had brought her, and taken a short walk around the garden, before sitting back down to review the second list of patients who required ongoing monitoring.

'Fine, thanks. I'm getting into the swing of things.'

Dan nodded, flopping into one of the chairs on the other side of the desk. She'd noticed that he preferred a more informal arrangement in his own consulting room, and wondered if he might help her move some of the furniture in here so that the desk didn't separate her from her patients.

'You've had lunch?'

Alice nodded, pushing the plate with the uneaten sandwich still on it towards him. 'Have you?'

'Molly's going to go out and get me something in a minute.' He reached forward, grabbing the sandwich and taking a hungry bite from it. 'Thanks.'

'You want a drink?' There was something intimate about sharing food in the moments between one task and the next. Like busy medical students, moulded into a team by a common purpose and loath to spend too much time in the cafeteria in case they missed something.

'I'll go...'

'*I'll* go. What flavour do you want?'

'Coffee flavour. Strong.' He grinned. 'Are you ready to go through the second list?'

'I'm ahead of you.' Alice smiled back. It had been a while since she'd been ahead of anyone or anything, and she savoured the thought as she picked up her mug and went to fetch Dan's from his desk.

Most of the list was straightforward. Patients who had recently been prescribed medication, and required a follow-up call. People who had recently been in hospital or required regular testing. The everyday work of the practice which sought to prevent a crisis rather than react to one. But there was one who made Alice think.

'Jasmine's seventeen—she's doing really well at school and loves sport. She's in the county netball team and plays football as well. She's been recovering from a complex break to her lower leg, and she's not doing as well as I'd hoped.' Dan frowned.

'How so?' Alice reread the report from the hospital. 'It says here that the procedure to stabilise the bone and implant an orthopaedic plate was a success.'

'Yes, it was. She did all that the physios asked of her when she was in hospital, but now she's home she seems to have lost interest. I've talked with her about her long-term prognosis, and told her that while she must avoid contact sports for a while, there's no reason why she can't maintain her level of fitness and that there's no one answer regarding what sports she'll be able to pursue at a high level once the bone's fully healed.'

Alice nodded. 'But it's all or nothing with her?'

'Very much so. When I tell her that we have to wait and see she gives me that look that teenagers are so good at. *You don't understand.*'

'And you think I might?' Alice wondered whether Dan might try to duck the question.

No chance. 'Your own experience of working to return to something you love is still raw at the moment and if you'd prefer not to share it then I'll keep Jasmine on my list. I just wanted to give her the opportunity to hear what you have to say, and you the opportunity to say it. If that's something you feel you're qualified for and ready to do.'

Dan had just given her a way out. Did he know that he'd helped to inspire her not to take it?

'I'm qualified. If she refuses to move I'll gently prod her in the ribs with my stick.'

He chuckled. 'You may have spoken too soon, that could turn out to be your only option. I was going to pop in on Jasmine to introduce you, and I can give you a lift there and back...?'

Alice looked at the address on the notes. 'I'll take a lift there, but I can walk back.'

'You're sure? You are on sick leave and I don't want anything you do here to compromise your own recovery.'

'It won't. Trust me, I know all of the good places to sit if I need a rest on the way.' Maybe she shouldn't have mentioned the T word. But Alice *did* want Dan to trust her.

'Okay, I'll take your word for it. Let me know when you're ready to go.'

'Whenever you are...'

Jasmine's family lived in a new house that had been built on the outskirts of the village. Dan accompanied her inside, and Jasmine's mother showed them into a large sitting room where floor-to-ceiling windows made the most of the surrounding countryside and gave a sense of space.

'Hi Jasmine. I'd like to introduce you to Dr Allenby. She'll be looking after you for the next few weeks.'

Jasmine smiled unenthusiastically. 'Okay.'

'Hello Jasmine. How are you doing?' Alice sat down in one of the comfortable chairs that Jasmine's mother had pointed them towards.

'Fine. I'll be going back to school when the new term starts.'

'That's in four weeks, isn't it? I'd expect so.' Alice smiled. There would be nothing to stop Jasmine from attending school now, if it wasn't the summer holidays. She wasn't going to congratulate her on going back to school in four weeks' time.

Her mother appeared to agree. 'You've already missed enough at school, Jasmine, and you won't be missing any more.'

'I *will* be, Mum. I've already missed the end of the current netball season, and no one seems to know when I'll be fit enough to start training again.'

'You could do other things. The physiotherapist said that gentle exercise would be fine…'

Jasmine turned the corners of her mouth down. This looked like a discussion she'd had before with her mother.

'Absolutely.' Alice stepped in to support Jasmine's mother. 'Have you done your physiotherapy exercises yet today, Jasmine?'

'No, not yet. I'll do them later.'

'I'd like to examine you *after* you've done your exercises, to see how you are then.' Alice glanced at Jasmine's mother. 'Perhaps I can come back in an hour?'

'Yes, of course, Doctor. Thank you.'

'All right then.' Alice got to her feet. 'I'll see you in an hour, Jasmine.'

Jasmine flipped her gaze towards Dan, as if he was going to save her from something. He smiled his usual smile—warm and reassuring—and followed Alice silently out into the hallway. Jasmine's mother stopped them at the front door.

'Dr Allenby, I'm so sorry to have wasted your time. I'll make sure that Jasmine does her exercises and is ready for you when you see her next.'

This was one person she wasn't going to have to persuade. Alice grinned. 'This isn't a waste of time at all. I want to make it clear to Jasmine that she's the one who needs to do the hard work involved in her recovery, I'm just here to observe and advise. I'm sure that you've been looking after Jasmine very well since her injury.'

'Running around after her, you mean.' Jasmine's mother gave a quiet smile. 'We all have, especially her father. He wants only the best for her, but perhaps we should be pushing her a little more?'

The way Dan had pushed her, when she'd needed it? 'Maybe you need to show her that she *can* do the things that she wants to. She may not be able to return to the high level of sporting achievement she's enjoyed just yet, and she might have to make a few decisions in the future, but she doesn't have to turn her back on sport entirely.'

'It's time to encourage her into doing the things she wants to do?'

'Yes. Exactly.'

Jasmine's mother nodded. 'I'll have a word with my husband tonight. I think this is just what Jasmine needs and we'll be supporting you in every way we can. Are you sure you have the time to come back later?'

'A supportive family is exactly what she needs right now, and I have a feeling you'll be doing far more work than I am. And coming back to make sure that Jasmine's done her exercises, and give her a few more challenges to think about, is what you need from me at the moment.'

'It's much appreciated.' Jasmine's mother reached out to shake Alice's hand. 'Excuse me for asking, but are you Dr Patrick Allenby's daughter?'

'Yes, I am.' Alice felt a shiver go up her spine. One that wasn't entirely one of foreboding.

'I'm so sorry for your loss. He was such a nice man, and everyone here remembers him with great affection.'

'Thank you.' Alice gripped her stick tightly,

wondering if her legs might suddenly give way beneath her. 'I appreciate that…'

Dan opened the passenger door of the car for her, closing it when Alice was settled in her seat. He seemed to be considering something as he walked around to the driver's seat.

'How did I do?' Alice pressed her lips together. She didn't usually exhibit that level of uncertainty over her patients. Perhaps the village was getting to her.

He shrugged. 'I could ask you the same question. Your approach is different. Let's see whether it works, where mine hasn't.'

Alice frowned. Having her own fears turned back at her wasn't the most comfortable reaction Dan could have offered. 'I'm sure you've been very supportive of Jasmine up till now, and you know as well as I do that kindness was exactly what she needed. You were the Nice Doctor, and you've got her to the point where she can fight back against the Nasty Doctor.'

'Nice of you to say so. I wouldn't call you nasty, exactly…' He grinned as Alice raised an eyebrow. 'Demanding, perhaps. In a good way. Where do you want to go now?'

'Is the bookshop still open? And do they still have a coffee corner?'

'Yes and yes. You feel like braving the village, then?'

'I don't have to trust them with my life to go and buy a book and read the first chapter over a coffee.' Alice was going to be out and about in the village, and she might as well face it now.

'Okay. I'll pick you up in an hour and bring you back here.' He leaned forward, starting the car.

'You don't need to.'

Dan shook his head. 'If you think I'm going to miss the next episode of this particular medical drama, then you're very much mistaken…'

CHAPTER SIX

IT HAD ONLY been a week. The slow and steady pace of the village didn't expect a man's life to change in a week.

Dan's life hadn't exactly changed—he did the same things every day. Ate breakfast with Charlie, then dropped him off at Eve Morrison's house while he went to work. Tussled with the medical ups and downs of what sometimes seemed like an unending stream of patients, and made his daily call to check on Tom Greene. Tom would be discharged soon and was planning to stay with his parents for a while to recuperate, then look for another job, close to where they lived in Edinburgh.

Then back to Eve's to pick Charlie up and hear about his day. Dan always made sure there was something for them to do together before dinner, and Charlie's bedtime meant that he had a couple of hours to spend working at home.

But Alice made it all special. She'd taken the evening surgery on Monday then come for dinner with Dan and Charlie, and in return insisted that she cook for them on Wednesday. It had been an exercise in how the everyday round of things-to-do could be turned into delight instead of routine. Dan had thought that contentment was enough, but Alice was making him happy.

She'd lightened the load on him at work, and her slightly unorthodox approach had been successful with several of the practice's patients. Alice had gone swimming on Thursday evening with Jasmine and her mum, and on Friday as he was leaving to pick up Charlie he saw Jasmine sitting in the waiting room alone.

'Hi Jasmine. You're waiting for Alice?'

'Yes. I've got some things to show her.' Jasmine laid her hand on the purple notebook in her lap, with a matching pen fixed to the cover. 'Mum brought me as far as the shops and I walked the rest of the way.'

'Right then. Good.' It appeared that Jasmine was beginning to take charge of her own recovery. 'I have to go and pick up Charlie but… I'll see you soon, no doubt?'

'Yes. You will.' Jasmine had a note of certainty in her voice which left Dan under no illusions that she and Alice were hatching plans together.

But on Saturday afternoon, when he and Charlie went to pick Alice up to take her shopping for food, it seemed that her determined steps forward had faltered. When Alice answered the door she was smiling, but her feet were bare on the polished floorboards and she was wearing a pair of old sweatpants and a T-shirt. There was something about her that seemed sad and lost. Charlie slipped his hand from Dan's and wrapped his arms around Alice's waist in a hug.

That was exactly what Dan wanted to do, but didn't dare…

'What's the matter?' Charlie asked the one and only question that was on Dan's mind. His version had been a little less insistent, and maybe he would have waited until everyone was sitting down, but Alice smiled, bending to curl one arm around the boy.

Her other hand was gripping the silver handle of her stick. 'Today seemed a little grey when I woke up. But now that you've brought the sunshine with you, I think it's going to be much more fun.'

Charlie nodded, obviously happy with her answer. 'Are we going to go now, Dad?'

'We'll wait until Alice is ready, shall we?'

She seemed to notice that she wasn't dressed to go out yet. 'Oh…yes. Sorry, I was looking through some things and lost track of time.'

'That's okay. Would you like me to make you a cup of tea?'

Alice nodded, obviously still caught up in the grey of her morning. 'Thanks, yes. There's some juice in the fridge for Charlie and his drawing book's in the sitting room…'

By the time Alice returned back downstairs, wearing a pair of loose cargo pants and a cotton top, Dan had made the tea and suggested that Charlie might like to draw a picture for Alice in the book she'd bought for his visit earlier in the week. It was Dan's turn to ask the question now.

'So, what *is* the matter.' Alice had sat down at the kitchen table and he put a mug of tea in front of her.

'It's nothing…'

Dan sat down opposite her. 'You knew that coming back here wasn't going to be easy. Why don't you give yourself a break?'

Alice took a sip of her tea. 'It's not important.'

'First it's nothing and now it's not important. You want me to get Charlie back in here to ask a few more of the hard questions?'

That made her smile. 'He might be busy. We shouldn't interrupt.'

'So talk to me instead.'

Maybe he was pushing Alice too hard. Dan had made out that his life was an open book, but there was one thing he'd never confided in her. If this was Alice's *one thing* then he ought to back off.

But she wiped her hand across her face, looking him straight in the eye. 'I walked down to the village this morning, and bumped into Mrs Harper. You know her?'

'Oh, yes. I know her.' Ella Harper had a sharp tongue, and she remembered pretty much everything that had gone on in the village for the last sixty years. 'What did she have to say for herself?'

'She told me she hadn't seen me since the car crash. Asked me if I'd been doing anything with myself since then.' Alice turned the corners of her mouth down. 'As if medical school and building a career with the air ambulance wasn't enough…'

Dan frowned. 'She knows what you've been doing. Patrick never missed an opportunity to brag about his talented daughter. You know how Ella is, she'll say anything to get a reaction.'

A little light crept across Alice's face. That was the reaction he wanted.

'Well, I smiled and said that I'd been keeping busy and she told me that she'd been wondering where I'd been hiding.' Alice shook her head. 'I know how she is, Dan, and that I'm not the only person she doesn't have a good word to say about. I knew I'd see her sooner or later and I walked back here thinking to myself that it hadn't been so bad but… I just couldn't settle. I decided that I had time to tidy the garden up a bit before you and Charlie came, then found myself crying over Dad's roses. He used to bring me roses from the garden when he came to visit.'

Alice's shoulders had slumped forward and suddenly she straightened her back. 'I thought I was handling this.'

'You are. Grief is… It sneaks up on you when you aren't expecting it.'

'But Dad's been gone for six months, now.'

'And you've been here for a week. Staying in Patrick's house, working at the practice that he built.' Dan made the obvious suggestion—the one that he was already dreading Alice would agree with. 'This is a lot. Maybe you should think about stepping back. Taking a little more time, and distance.'

'You want me to?'

Dan couldn't give anything but an honest answer. 'No.'

'I don't want to either. However hard it is, this is the place I need to be, if I'm ever going to move forward. And I'm really grateful for all of the support you've given me.'

It was ironic. Dan *had* been determined to do all that he could to make Alice's stay easier. At first, he'd done it for Patrick's sake, but now that he'd fallen under her spell it was all for her. And the truth was that helping her to confront all of the things she'd been trying to avoid would only make it easier for her to move on with her life and leave.

He couldn't change that. All he could do was to take the here and now. By the scruff of its neck if necessary. He reached forward, the tips of his fingers touching hers.

It felt as if a switch had been flipped, completing a circuit. Sweet electricity began to flow between them. If Alice didn't feel this too…

She felt it. He could see it in her eyes, the golden shards suddenly alive with light. She reached forward, slipping her hand into his. 'You always make me feel better about things, Dan.'

'That's not my intention. Feeling better isn't always a way forward, you know that.' He smiled at her. Dan didn't understand how anyone could keep themselves from smiling when Alice was around, even Ella Harper.

'To be honest…' Alice's gaze told him that her honesty might just be brutal '…it wasn't all about Ella. She just got me thinking. I did something that I'm not very proud of.'

'So what? Doesn't that just make you human?' Dan swallowed hard. If Alice wanted to confide in him there was no way he wanted to stop her, but it raised a serious question. If she could tell him all of her secrets, then why couldn't he tell his?

If Alice was ever going to move forward, she needed to break the mould. Stop running, and stand her ground. Only right now, it wasn't her injured knee that was stopping her from running, it was the warmth that lingered in Dan's eyes.

'When I was injured… It was two weeks after Dad's funeral. I had a lot on my mind, I knew I had to come back here and sort everything out and… I didn't want to think about it. I didn't want to think about how much I missed Dad either, and I'd told everyone that I was fine being back on active service. It was what he would have wanted…'

She'd let go of his hand, and was hugging her arms around her stomach.

Dan narrowed his eyes. 'Okay. I can understand the feeling, that you just want things to return to some semblance of normal. But my impression was that the funeral didn't give you any closure.'

'No. It's supposed to, isn't it?'

'I think it's more a matter of helping you start that process. And I'm honestly not sure that Patrick would have wanted you to rush it.'

Alice knew that he wouldn't. Someone had to say that, and since Dan had, she didn't need to. 'We had a call out to a traffic accident on the motorway. We'd already made one trip, taking the most badly injured to the hospital, and we had to go back. The police had established a cordon around the spot where we'd previously landed, as it was close to a service station and people had come out to see the helicopter. That's a hazard we have to watch out for—the helicopter catches everyone's attention.'

Dan nodded. 'And sometimes they get in the way?'

'Rarely. But sometimes we have to clear people back when we take off. They move back out of the way of the blades, but don't think about the down-draught. If the police are there then they usually handle it. We landed okay, and everyone stood back for us to get the injured man aboard…'

Alice heard a clatter coming from the sitting room and fell silent. A moment later, Charlie ran into the kitchen, holding a sheet of paper in front of him.

'Dad! I drew Alice and the helicopter…'

Dan grinned suddenly, examining the picture Charlie had drawn. 'Again? Although I think this is the best one yet.'

The tension in the room seemed to dissipate suddenly. Alice felt like crying with relief. 'Can I see, Charlie?'

Charlie nodded. 'It's for you.'

She smiled at the boy, giving him a hug. 'Thank you! It's beautiful. Shall I put it on my fridge door with the others?' She nodded towards the large fridge-freezer, where the pictures that Charlie had drawn for her when he and Dan had come to dinner were proudly displayed.

'Yes!' Charlie liked the idea, and Dan nudged his son conspiratorially.

'There's going to be space for one more. What do you think?'

Charlie nodded, turning wordlessly and running back to the sitting room. Dan turned to her.

'He's got such great timing. Are you thinking it's going to let you off the hook?'

Alice felt tears in her eyes. 'Maybe I was hoping so.'

Dan rose wordlessly from his seat, coming to sit down on the chair next to her. Then he laid his arm across the back of her seat. Gentle, warm and… Suddenly, clinging to him was the one and only thing that Alice wanted to do. For a little comfort maybe, but then…

It would have been a nice diversion, something to make her forget about the past and the future, and the troubles that lay between the two. But the pleasure of a stolen kiss wouldn't solve anything.

She removed her hand from the sleeve of his shirt, where her fingers had mysteriously become entangled. Then took a breath.

'The doors were closed and the pilot was powering up the blades. Then I saw a little girl sneaking under the cordon and running towards us. I shouted that we weren't clear for take-off, but not quickly enough, and the downwash lifted her off her feet and then slammed her down onto the ground. She was trying to get up and I opened the doors and ran to get her.'

'And no one else had seen her?'

'No one on the helicopter, she was out of everyone else's line of sight. The police had their backs to us, watching the crowd, but there was a paramedic from one of the ambulances on the scene who saw. He was too far away, though. I got knocked off my feet—that was when I injured my knee—but somehow, I managed to crawl to the little girl and get hold of her.'

'And this was…anything other than an act of bravery on your part?' Dan looked perplexed.

'It was thoughtless. I acted on my own without telling anyone what I was about to do. As a result of that I was injured and we lost time in getting our patient back to the hospital. And the team lost its doctor.'

'But you saved a little girl from potential injury. That matters.'

'Yes, it does. But we're a team, that's how we operate most effectively. All I was thinking about was myself and that running and grabbing that little girl might somehow alleviate the pain I was in over Dad's death. Don't you understand, Dan?' Alice couldn't bear it if he didn't.

He nodded slowly. 'Yeah, I get it. You think you made the decision for the wrong reasons. That doesn't mean it was the wrong decision, does it?'

'I hope that the rest of the team see it that way and they want me back…' If they didn't, Alice wasn't sure what she would do.

'Someone said this to you?' Dan frowned.

'No, and I wasn't in a position to listen for a while. I told the A&E doctors that I wanted as much pain relief as they could give me. I said it to myself, though.'

'And what else did you say?'

This was what had hurt more than her knee had. 'That I'd run away from the village, and now I was running away from Dad's death. That I hadn't been honest when I'd said I was fine and ready for active service, and we could have got to the little girl faster and more safely if I hadn't been so absorbed in my own troubles. Maybe it's just as well that I'm not fit for duty physically…'

Alice almost choked on the words. She'd been trying to dispel those doubts, telling everyone that she couldn't wait to be passed as physically fit, but in her heart of hearts wondering whether she still had what it took to rejoin her team.

'I think…' Dan was clearly choosing his words carefully. 'Everything that had been happening in your life didn't cloud your judgement; it made you question yourself. If I could choose someone who'd be there for Charlie in a moment of danger and I couldn't be there, I'd want it to be you.'

Alice felt tears spill from her eyes. It was what she wanted to hear more than anything. What she dared not believe.

'I mean it, Alice.' She felt his arm move to her shoulders, comforting her, and she struggled for control. 'I wouldn't say that if I didn't believe it.'

If Dan could trust her that much… Alice gave in, leaning towards him and sobbing on his shoulder. 'I'm sorry, I…'

'It's okay.' He was solid. Comforting. Dan let her cry until she'd run out of tears and was ready to straighten her back and put everything back together again. 'What happens next?'

'What do you mean?'

'I came here—ran here, actually—because I didn't want to repeat the mistakes that Nola and I had made. I wanted to be there for Charlie every day, for him to know that he can depend on me.'

'You two are a team.' Alice was beginning to see what she had to do next. 'You'd do anything to keep from losing him.'

'Yes, I would. You left the village because you felt that people didn't trust you. You've made a different life for yourself, and maybe you need to think differently now. Don't assume that people can't trust you; give them the benefit of the doubt and ask how they feel. Is there someone you can ask?'

'Yes, asking's no problem. What if I don't get the answer I want?'

'I don't think that's going to happen. If it does, then at least you'll know and we can work on it.'

We'll work on it? Was Alice part of Dan and Charlie's team now? If that was the case then he'd obviously put out a silent call for his second-in-command, because Charlie came bursting through the door, another drawing clutched to his chest.

'I made you another one…'

Alice admired the picture, which was of a helicopter, with three large faces. 'That's me.' Charlie pointed helpfully to the face at the front. 'I'm taking you and Dad for a ride in my helicopter. When I grow up and learn to fly one.'

'That's beautiful, Charlie. I'm looking forward to that.' Alice rearranged the magnets on the fridge door, removing her shopping list and putting the new drawing in pride of place.

'In the meantime, we can go to the supermarket.' Dan reached for the list in Alice's hand and turned to Charlie. 'Alice has some things to do, so we'll see her later when we bring her shopping back.'

'You're doing my shopping?'

Dan's smooth, relentless motion in propelling himself and Charlie from the kitchen to the front door stopped for a moment. 'Don't you have some calls to make?'

She had one call, and she was currently wondering how long she could put that off. It looked as if Dan wasn't having any of that.

'All right. I want *chocolate* biscuits…'

He nodded, sweeping Charlie towards the front door, leaving Alice alone.

CHAPTER SEVEN

MAYBE DAN HAD been a little high-handed about this. He considered the matter as he stood in front of the display of fruit in the supermarket. Alice had written *Fruit* on her list, obviously intending to choose when she got here.

'What shall we get for Alice, Charlie?'

Charlie didn't need to think. 'Bananas.'

'Okay.' Dan put two large bunches of bananas into the trolley, one for Alice and one for Charlie. 'Anything else?'

Charlie shook his head, and Dan decided to get a selection. Anything that Alice didn't want, he'd take.

Had he been too pushy? Expected too much of her? A week ago, he'd been cautious, expecting nothing of Alice and intent on giving her as much time as she needed. But Dan just couldn't stand by and watch her injury take away the job that she loved.

If she hadn't called anyone while they were out shopping, then maybe he should leave it alone and back off a little. He wasn't in charge of Alice's life, and he had no right to tell her what to do with it, even if he was drawn to her like a moth to a flame.

That was easy to think while he and Charlie were in the supermarket, and much harder to contemplate when he parked outside Alice's house and he saw her standing in the doorway as if she'd been waiting for them. Dan started to unload the shopping from the car, giving Charlie the bag that contained just chocolate biscuits and bananas. Charlie ran to Alice, receiving a wide smile and a *thank-you.*

Perhaps that studied cheerfulness of hers meant that she hadn't called anyone. Or maybe she had, and had heard something she didn't want to in reply to her questions. Or perhaps she'd called and never plucked up the courage to ask… There were too many permutations to think about and Dan had promised himself that he wasn't going to push her.

'I called Toby, the chief pilot on our team, while you were out.' She made it sound like a *by-the-way* as she took two mugs from the kitchen cupboard, put the kettle on for tea and broke a banana from the bunch, giving it to Charlie.

'Yes?' Dan concentrated on unpacking the rest of her shopping onto the kitchen table.

'I suppose you don't want to hear what we talked about, then?'

Studied indifference could only be taken so far. Especially when he could feel Alice's golden gaze on him. Dan turned.

'I give in. What did he say?'

'I asked him whether he thought I'd been out of line when I was injured, and he didn't know what I was talking about. They want me back, Dan. He says that their new medic is a really nice guy and he's good at what he does, but he's only been assigned to them until I'm back and he's already decided that his long-term future doesn't lie with the air ambulance service…' Alice grinned broadly. 'He said that they're all hoping for some good news when I go for my medical.'

'That's great. What you wanted to hear?'

'Yes. When I told Toby how I'd been feeling he said *all* the things I wanted to hear. Are you going to tell me that you told me so?'

'I'm not sure that I did, did I?'

'What did Dad tell you?' Charlie piped up.

Alice grinned at him. 'Your dad told me that it was worth taking a risk for something I really wanted.'

Dan wasn't sure whether he'd actually voiced that thought, but Alice had got the message. He leaned over, grabbing the banana skin that Charlie was about to put back into one of the shopping bags and threw it into the recycling bin.

When he turned, Alice's gaze was still on him. There was more to say, but maybe not when Charlie was within earshot. 'What do you say we go and get something to eat and then go somewhere this afternoon? Celebrate a little.'

'We could go swimming? That's really good exercise for my knee.' She grinned at him impishly.

'The pool's always really crowded on Saturdays, it's better to go early mornings. But we could check out the gym, I think membership there includes entrance to the pool.'

'Yes, okay.' Alice was still smiling as she started to pack the shopping away.

The gym was light and airy, and ideal for the modified exercise programme that Alice had devised to take her injury into account. There was a supervised soft play area and the glass partition between that and the main gym meant that Dan could keep an eye on Charlie.

'You're thinking of joining me then?' Alice asked him.

'I might do. I've been too busy for the gym lately, and I let my subscription lapse. This place is much nicer than the one I used to go to.'

It was a good thought. If her enthusiasm flagged then it was bound to be reawakened by some sweat on Dan's brow. He was in good shape, but she reckoned that exercise gear might make his shoulders a lot more easy on the eye, too.

'But—are you any less busy now?' Alice wasn't

sure that her contribution would be enough to make up for the loss of Dr Greene.

He grinned. 'I've got a plan…'

She'd learned to expect that. 'Okay. What have you got up your sleeve? Twenty handkerchiefs knotted together? A white dove?' Charlie didn't get the joke and grabbed his father's arm, trying to roll the sleeve of his casual shirt up a little further to find out.

'A friend of Patrick's gave me a call the other day—he'd heard that Dr Greene had been taken ill and that the practice was struggling to cope. Did Patrick ever mention Dr John McIntyre to you?'

'Yes, he did. Dad met him at a conference. He's a GP in Cambridge but he has his finger in a lot of other pies. He's just retired, hasn't he?'

'Yes, about a year ago. He and his wife moved to Silverton, to be closer to their daughter. John's offered to help out with a couple of days a week of his time, which will allow us a lot more flexibility. And since we're not paying you, I think the least we can do is make sure you have time off whenever you need it… Okay, Charlie. I don't *really* have any doves hidden up my sleeve.'

Charlie seemed disappointed at the omission, and turned his attention to the glass partition that separated them from the soft play area.

'But when can *I* come?' Clearly, he was feeling a little left out.

'You can come at the weekends, Charlie. I have to exercise every day. And it's better for me to do it here than at home,' Alice told him.

'And better during the morning or at lunchtime, rather than when you're tired after a day's work,' Dan added. 'One of the conditions of you working at the practice is that it doesn't get in the way of your rehab.'

Alice turned the corners of her mouth down. Today seemed to be her day for awkward confessions. 'That'll be a little more than what I'm currently doing, actually.'

'Really?' Dan didn't look even slightly surprised. In fact, he was trying to hide a smile.

'Are you this devious with your patients, Dan?'

'More so.' He grinned. 'Patrick taught me well.'

'Clearly, I need a little more than a week to get me back up to speed with Dad's approach to anyone who got in the way of his grand plan to keep everyone in the village healthy.' Talking about her father with someone else who'd clearly cared about him and respected him was a warm feeling. So different from the sudden weight around her heart that had accompanied her thoughts of him for the last six months.

'So I'll sign us both up for a month, shall I?'

'Um…how much is it?'

'I'll take care of it. Call it part of our commitment to your recovery.'

Alice rather liked this side of him. Dan's gentle, easygoing approach to the world concealed a very stubborn streak, and she was learning that he was stubborn about all of the right things.

'You're not leaving me much choice, Dan. I'm going to have to stop off at the gym shop and buy one of those T-shirts to show my commitment to this, I didn't pack for exercising in public.' Every other person here seemed to be wearing a smart, well-fitting top with the gym's name printed on one sleeve.

He nodded, his slow smile spreading across his face. 'The blue's nice. Or the green…'

Everything seemed to be falling into place. Alice's daily exercises weren't quite a pleasure, but she felt that she had a goal now and that they would get her there. Being here, surrounded by all of the things that were part of her father's life, was still hard but she was learning how to smile at the memories. Gaining a measure of closure.

And the people at the surgery were becoming friends. They wished her a good morning, and knew how she took her coffee. On Monday morning Molly had asked what she'd been up to at the weekend, and Alice had told her that she'd joined a gym.

'Oh, which one?'

'The new one, on the other side of Silverton. It's really nice there.'

'I know the one.' Molly smiled. 'So you'll be doing your rehab there?'

'I'm planning to. Somehow, it's easier to find the motivation for it when you're not at home.'

Molly laughed, nodding. 'Don't I know it. I go to a fitness class once a week, and without it I don't think I'd do anything. Apart from running around after my very own model railway enthusiast, that is. There always seems to be something on, and I enjoy the trips out and seeing the regulars at the meet-ups, even if I'm not much interested in the trains.'

'That counts as exercise. Is that what you were up to at the weekend?'

'No, I wish it had been.' Molly rolled her eyes. 'It's my fiftieth birthday in less than a fortnight. I thought I'd make a thing of it because…why not, eh? I'm having it at the Swan Inn and they'll take care of the food and drink but they want to know numbers, so I've been phoning around all weekend to see who'll be there.' Molly leaned forward across the counter. 'I'd love it if you could come. It's on Friday week and you don't have to stay all evening, but we'll be having cake and champagne at around seven-thirty. And everyone from the surgery will be there.'

Molly must know that something had happened to keep Alice away from the village, even if she didn't know the details. And if Alice was completely honest the thought of the pub in the centre of the village, packed full of people that she'd been avoiding ever since she was nineteen, didn't fill her with much enthusiasm. But it was kind of Molly to ask and she smiled back. 'Thanks. I'll certainly try.'

'Please do. It'll be lovely to see you there.'

'I'm still not sure about whether to go or not…'

It was Friday afternoon. Alice had gone to the gym early this morning, and an unexpected free hour, after a very busy week, had allowed them to take a walk by the river that ran past the surgery before Dan had to be back for his evening appointments. And this was the third time that Alice had brought the subject up since Molly had invited her to the party.

Clearly, it had been dwelling on her mind. Dan had told her that it wasn't obligatory, that Molly would understand if she didn't go, or she didn't stay long. They could go together if she liked. He quite liked the idea of walking into a party with Alice by his side, but put that pleasure aside in favour of the greater purpose of chasing away anyone who approached Alice with the sole intention of raking up the past.

'There's always the surprise we're planning for her on Thursday, so it's not as if Friday's your only opportunity to wish her a happy birthday.' Morning coffee with cake, a present and a card, signed by everyone.

But Alice was still fretting about the party, and it had nothing to do with anything he could suggest. It was all about the village, and a hurt that wouldn't go away.

Dan glanced up at the trees bending over their heads to shade the path running by the stream. No answers there.

'You could forget about it for a week, and make your decision next Friday evening.' He turned to her, seeing her frown. 'I know that's a lot to ask.'

'It's…yes, it is a lot to ask. What am I going to wear?'

'Any one of the outfits I've seen you in this last week at work. Or the week before… It's a come-as-you-are kind of thing.' Dan knew that there wasn't much point in telling her that she always looked gorgeous. If Alice was going to face her fears then she probably wanted the confidence of knowing she looked spectacular.

'Tomorrow's Saturday. We can go to the gym and then do a bit of shopping if you like.' It was all that Dan could think of to suggest.

'Do you mind?' Alice looked up at him thoughtfully. 'Hitting the shops for a dress probably isn't your first choice of things to do on a Saturday. Or Charlie's.'

One thing that he'd learned about Alice was that honesty was sometimes more helpful than tact. Now was one of those times.

'If you're wondering whether it'll bring back

memories…' He shrugged. 'Maybe it will, lots of things do. That's something about my life that I've learned to accept, for my own sake as well as Charlie's. It's not a bad thing any more.'

Alice smiled. 'In that case, some company and a second opinion would be very welcome.'

'So that's settled? Shopping tomorrow, present giving on Thursday and we'll go with the flow on Friday.'

Dan had forgotten how much he'd liked these easy negotiations. Being part of a life that didn't involve the loss he'd experienced in both his childhood and with Nola's death. Maybe even being able to love again, but that was a little *too* honest, too uncertain a thought for him to share, even with himself.

'It's settled until about ten minutes before we leave for the party on Friday. Then I might be panicking…'

'That's okay. Next Friday's a long way away.' Now, there was a sunny afternoon, and Alice had slipped her hand into the crook of his arm. Maybe steadying herself, but the way that Dan didn't have to offer and Alice didn't have to ask was all part of the companionship that had flourished between them.

Up ahead, a group of children were fishing from a nearby bridge, and a little further down two women were sitting in the sunshine on the riverbank, watching them. Alice nodded towards the children.

'Dad used to take me fishing from that bridge all the time. We never caught anything but I used to love just listening to him talk. Telling me how water flows down from the hills to make a river, and how trees grow…'

'He used to take Charlie, and they never came back with any fish either. But they both used to like going.' Dan gestured towards one of the women. 'Do you remember Elaine…?'

'Elaine…?' Alice gazed at her and then nodded. 'Yes, of course—you could never miss her red hair. She's a bit older than me and we didn't have much to do with each other as kids… She's married now, with children?'

'Yep. You probably won't know her friend—Geeta and her husband are new to the village… Not as new as me, they were here when I arrived. Geeta's one of Charlie's teachers at school.'

Dan felt Alice's fingers tighten on his arm as a small boy started to climb the low parapet of the bridge. Elaine called to him.

'Evan, what did I say? No climbing…'

The warning seemed to serve as an encouragement for the boy and he leaned over the parapet, looking at the water flowing below him, probably trying to see if there really were any fish to catch. Evan's little brother Davey followed suit and the two of them started to play-fight, laughing and pushing each other. Dan quickened his pace, leaving Alice behind and starting to run towards the bridge.

CHAPTER EIGHT

TOO LATE. The boys were on their feet on the wide parapet, their arms flung towards the summer sky in an expression of mastery of everything around them. Then they jumped.

It wasn't the fall that made Dan rush to the riverbank. Even in summertime, the water would be more than just cool and refreshing—it was cold enough to make anyone feel a severe jolt. That jolt was a quickening of the heart and a sudden rise in blood pressure, and it would provoke an involuntary gasp, drawing water into the lungs. He'd made sure that there were posters up in the surgery and at the local school, warning about cold water shock, but the difficulty was just this. A warm summer's day which made the water seem so inviting.

As he waded into the water, he could see that Evan had surfaced. He was in trouble, splashing and choking. But Davey was drifting motionless, under the water.

It was a choice he didn't have to make. Alice

was there, just behind him and making for Evan. Dan took a breath, ducking his head beneath the surface, and grabbed Davey, lifting him carefully out of the water.

‘Okay…?’ he called to Alice, who had reached Evan and was calming him, using the water to support his weight as she moved him towards the riverbank.

‘Yes. Go.’

He needed to trust her now. Know that Evan was safe in Alice’s care, while he attended to Davey. Dan turned, wading back towards the water’s edge.

‘Evan… Davey…’ Elaine and Geeta were sprinting towards them, and Dan heard panic in Elaine’s voice as she cried out her sons’ names.

‘Elaine, stay where you are and help Alice lift Evan out of the water… Geeta, get the other kids off the bridge…’ He needed Elaine to stop panicking and focus on what had to be done next.

‘Do as Dan says…’ Geeta grabbed her friend by the shoulders, giving her a not-too-gentle shake, and Elaine calmed suddenly, bending down as Alice neared the riverbank with Evan. Geeta ran towards the other children, herding them off the bridge while Dan carried Davey to a firm, flat piece of ground and laid him gently down on his back.

He could feel the sun on the nape of his neck as he tilted Davey’s chin up and backwards, clearing the boy's mouth with his finger. For one long moment neither doctor or patient breathed, and then Davey's chest began to rise and fall and he started to choke, river water running from his mouth. When the boy began to retch Dan turned him onto his side, carefully maintaining his airway and soothing him as best he could.

Alice and Elaine had got Evan out of the water now, and he heard Alice talking to someone on the phone. Then she called to him.

'Molly's phoning the emergency services—they'll be on their way soon…'

For a moment, Alice's gaze met his, and she nodded silently. Dan returned her nod and then shifted his attention back to the boy in his care. He and Alice had said all that they needed to and he could leave her to deal with Evan while he concentrated on Davey.

'Need anything?' Geeta called across to him, from where the rest of the children were sitting, obviously under strict instructions not to move.

'The rugs you were sitting on. Jackets, sweaters…anything that's dry and will keep them warm. Half to me, half to Alice…' The shock of the cold water would have constricted both boys' surface blood vessels as their bodies attempted to preserve core heat, and even though they were out of the water now, the risk of hypothermia still remained.

Geeta responded quickly. By the time Dan had gently removed Davey's T-shirt she had handed him a sweatshirt that was a little too big for him, but warm and easy to slip over his head. Then Dan could take off Davey's wet jeans and wrap him in the rug that lay by his side.

'Okay. You're okay, Davey. I know you're scared, but you're safe now and everything's going to be all right. Try to lie still.' He curled his arms around the boy, for both reassurance and warmth, and felt Davey's breathing become slower and steadier. 'That's great. Well done, you're doing really well.'

'Mum…'

Dan looked up and saw two heads turn towards him in response to Davey's tremulous call. Alice was busy with Evan, getting him out of his wet clothes, and she nodded to Elaine. 'Go to him. I'll look after Evan.' She gestured to Geeta to come and help her wrap Evan up warm.

'Try to keep him still and reassure him.' Dan smiled at Elaine, who was trembling as she knelt down next to Davey.

'I should have been there—'

'Being here for him now is all that matters.'

Elaine nodded, curling her arms around her son. 'Davey. Sweetheart… Everything's all right.'

'Mum…' Davey snuggled against her, trying to extricate his hand from the folds of the rug. Dan carefully laid him back down, wrapping the rug around both of them so that the boy could feel his mother's warmth.

He felt a sudden jolt of regret at the thought that Charlie didn't remember how it felt to have his mother comfort him, and that now he would never know. Dan pushed it aside, checking on Davey yet again.

He heard the tone of a phone, and absent-mindedly pulled his own phone from his back pocket. The screen was blank and it was dripping wet, but when he looked towards Alice she had hers against her ear. She ended the call and spoke to Geeta, then turned to Dan, smiling at him.

'That was Molly, the ambulance will be here in ten minutes. Geeta's going up to the road to wait for them and point them in our direction.'

Geeta had got to her feet and was arranging the four other children in a line, two on either side of her, all holding hands. She flashed Alice a grin and set off on the path that would take them up onto the main road.

'How's Evan?' Dan asked, and Alice nodded, glancing down at the boy.

'He didn't breathe in any water when he gasped, and he's starting to get warm now. You're feeling a bit better Evan?'

Evan managed a smile. 'Yes. Is Davey all right?'

Alice nodded. 'He's looking much better… How's he doing, Dr Ryan?'

Her use of *Dr Ryan* was calculated to reassure Evan, even though Dan knew the family and Evan was well aware that he was a doctor. 'He's a lot better. Doing well, Evan.'

Evan seemed to want to see for himself, but Alice quieted him, keeping him still and warm in the rug that was wrapped around him.

'Thank you,' Elaine murmured. 'You must be wet through…'

Dan had hardly thought about that. 'I'm drying off. The ambulance should be here in ten minutes…' There was something that Elaine needed before it arrived. 'You did so well, Elaine.'

'I panicked…' Her voice was just a whisper now.

'Of course you did. If it had been Charlie, I would have done exactly the same. But you got yourself together and helped—your boys can be very proud of their mum.'

A tear ran down Elaine's cheek as she stroked Davey's face gently. 'Thanks, Dan. That means a lot. I'm so grateful that you and Alice were here…'

Dan forced himself to relax, smiling at Elaine. 'So am I.'

They weren't just words of reassurance for a mother whose worst nightmare had just broken the peace of a sunny day. Dan had trusted Alice to do what was necessary, and she'd trusted him. Whatever they did with that trust remained to be seen.

It was less than ten minutes before the ambulance crew appeared, carrying their bags through the trees. They quickly checked on the two boys and then went back to their vehicle to fetch two cots. Dan helped carry the boys to the ambulance and Elaine climbed in after them. Geeta was taking the other children home with her and would look after Elaine's little girl.

Dan walked back to the riverside and found Alice sitting in the sunshine, waiting for him. He sat down next to her.

'They're on their way?'

'Yes. I imagine they'll both be staying in hospital overnight, just to make sure there are no after-effects. Particularly Davey, he had quite a bit of water on his lungs.' Delayed drowning could be caused by water irritating the lungs, leading to a build-up of fluid. It was rare, but could occur as much as twenty-four hours after a near-drowning event.

'They're safe now, though.' Alice lay back on the grass, staring at the sky. 'And it's a beautiful day. I could almost stay here to dry off…' She turned her head towards him. 'Or I could ask you what's bugging you.'

Right now, Dan could almost see himself telling her. 'Nothing.'

Alice pursed her lips. 'Are you going to give "*It's okay*" a miss?'

He trusted Alice enough to hear this. Maybe he always had, and it had taken a while for him to realise it. 'Those boys. They were so afraid. I know just what that's like.'

Alice put two and two together. 'You were afraid when you were a child?'

'I was… Did I tell you that I was adopted when I was four?' Dan was struggling now, wondering how to put something that he never talked about into words.

'I think you know that you didn't.' Alice sat up, golden warmth flashing in her eyes. 'Your adoptive family weren't kind?'

'They were wonderful. I have a mum and dad, two brothers and a sister, and Charlie loves them as much as I do.'

'Your biological family, then?' Alice was there with him, trying to give him the words that Dan was struggling for.

'I don't remember much about my biological parents. But I remember being afraid. Being hungry…' The feeling almost swamped Dan, and he felt Alice's hand take his. Pulling him back, out of the swirling waters of the past.

'Much later, I asked my dad what had happened. He told me that my biological parents used to go out a lot, leaving me alone at home. Once they left me for days. The neighbours called the police when they heard me crying, and they found me curled up on the sofa, in dirty clothes and surrounded by sweet papers and empty sandwich wrappers. When my biological parents came back and realised that they were in trouble, they disappeared.'

'Oh, Dan… I'm so sorry that happened to you, no child should have to go through that.' Alice squeezed his hand. 'And when you met your wife, you thought that you wouldn't be alone again…'

All of the pieces suddenly fell into place. Dan had known, but it had taken Alice to put it into words. How his childhood fears had fed his grief for Nola, and his determination that Charlie would always feel loved and protected.

'I guess so. Things didn't happen that way though.'

'Is that what makes Mallory Cross so important? It's not just a matter of being able to spend more time with Charlie, although that's always a good thing. You can build a life here. Make Charlie feel safe, and that he'll never be alone.'

Dan stared at Alice. 'That's how *I* feel about it. But it's not your experience…'

Alice shrugged. 'No, it isn't. But we all make our own places of safety. Mine's just different to yours.'

And that was why they couldn't be together.

Alice had put that into words, too, and somehow it didn't seem quite such an absolute now. More a problem that, given a bit of time and thought, might be solved.

Alice's phone rang and she turned the corners of her mouth down. 'Sorry, it's the surgery.' She listened for a minute, and then smiled.

'I'll ask.' She turned to Dan. 'It's John McIntyre. Molly's called him in to do your evening surgery. He wants to know if either of us have any cuts or abrasions.'

Dan shook his head. 'I don't. I didn't swallow any water either. You?'

'No.' Alice relayed the information to John, and listened to what was clearly a list of instructions. 'Okay, yes, we will… Yes, the boys will both be at the hospital now… Thanks, John, it's really appreciated.' She ended the call.

'What was all that about?' Dan asked.

'Apparently Molly phoned John and told him that we'd been wading around in the river, and he offered to do your evening surgery for you. He's there now, and just wanted to reinforce the warnings about wading around in rivers. He's going to take our word for it on the cuts and abrasions, as a professional courtesy, and says that we're both to go home and get ourselves cleaned up. John's such a sweetheart…'

Dan chuckled. 'Don't let him hear you say that.' John's brand of caring was always kindly, but he could be forthright when he felt he needed to. 'Do you think he'll find out if we stay here for another five minutes?'

'I won't tell if you don't. Is your phone not working?'

Dan pulled it out of his pocket, shaking it, and several drops of water flew out. 'I think it's well and truly waterlogged. Yours is okay?'

'Yes, I dropped it on the riverbank before I went in. I've had that happen before.'

'Good thinking.' Dan leaned back on his elbows, looking at the sky. 'Do you suppose...?'

Alice looked round at him questioningly when he didn't finish. 'Give me a clue, Dan.'

'I was just wondering...whether we'll always be so bound by the past.'

Alice thought about it for a moment. 'No. Or probably yes, but maybe not. It isn't straightforward...'

Dan chuckled. 'I'll be honest and say that I was hoping for a more definitive answer.'

'Then you should ask easier questions.' Alice nudged her arm against his shoulder.

A thought hit him and Dan looked around. 'Where's your stick?'

Alice grimaced. 'I was wondering when you'd notice. I dropped that on the riverbank with my phone. Seems I don't need it as much as I think I do.'

Dan thought for a moment, not wanting to express an opinion. 'I suppose…adrenaline? How's your knee now?'

'Fine. I still can't bend it any further than before, but it feels…strong.'

Dan nodded. Alice seemed stronger, too. As if the prospect of returning to her team had given her purpose.

'Thanks for not saying that I was probably just leaning on it for emotional support.' She wrinkled her nose in a frown.

'I wasn't going to. When you've been using something for as long as you've needed the stick, it can become a habit. I dare say that you'd have left it behind at some point.'

Alice chuckled. 'That sounds much better. I'll take your diagnosis, Dr Ryan, even if I'm not sure whether you're just being kind.'

Maybe he was. But Alice was so hard on herself, so unforgiving, that it just restored a balance. 'You could try it some time. Being a little kinder.'

'I'm kind!' she protested, and Dan laughed.

'You're *very* kind—to everyone else. Not so much to yourself. What do you say we pick up Charlie and you come to mine and let me cook you dinner?'

'I was thinking that you and Charlie could come to mine for a takeaway. Pizza seems just right for a Friday evening spent doing nothing.'

'Let's compromise. Pizza at my place, because Charlie has more to entertain him there. He might decide that he wants a quiet evening in with a film.'

'Cartoons? I could really get into a few cartoons right now. Something not too demanding...'

Dan seemed as reluctant to move as Alice was. They sat in the sun, silent for a few minutes. Time with him seemed to slip through her fingers, precious but fluid. Gone far too soon.

He got to his feet, walking to the water's edge to pick up her stick, where it had lain forgotten. But when he helped Alice up, he offered her his arm and she took it.

'Aren't you afraid that I might swap one thing to lean on for another?' Alice looked up at him. His clothes were still wet and grimy from the river, and Dan was clearly weary, but he'd never seemed so handsome. Someone who didn't hesitate in running into a river to save a child.

'No. I trust you to be stronger than that.'

Was that a challenge? Alice decided that it probably was because, despite his easygoing, relaxed air, Dan was one of the most challenging people she'd ever met.

They walked back to the surgery to collect Dan's car and Alice was unable to stop him from popping his head around the door and thanking Molly for all she'd done that afternoon.

'It's my pleasure. I'm glad those two little boys are all right.'

'Will you pass on my thanks to John as well? I really appreciate his doing my evening surgery.'

Molly fixed Dan with a fierce smile. 'Of course I will. Off with you both before you start dripping on the carpet.' She snapped the sliding window that separated her office from the reception area shut, in a clear indication that this was her last word on the subject.

Alice could see Molly watching them out to the car through her office window. She waved as he fumbled with the keys before starting the engine.

'Let's go before they change their minds. Or before they don't and they call the police to escort us off the premises.' She summoned a smile and gave Molly a wave back.

Dan chuckled, manoeuvring around John's car and out of the driveway. Alice leaned back in her seat, closing her eyes. 'Why am I so tired all of a sudden? It's not as if I haven't done this kind of thing before.'

'It's been a busy week already, on every front imaginable. And now we've been told in no uncertain terms to go home and relax. That'll do it every time, won't it?'

'Yes, it will. You must be tired, too.' Dan had been spending time with John McIntyre, getting him up to speed, as well as covering for her trips to the gym and seeing a constant stream of patients.

He shot her that relaxed smile of his. 'Wait until Charlie's asleep in bed. *Then* I might start yawning…'

They stopped outside Eve Morrison's house, and Alice waited by the car as Dan strode up the front path. Those few moments when Charlie ran out to hug him belonged to the two of them alone. But today, Charlie stopped suddenly before flinging himself into his father's arms.

'You're all wet, Dad!' the boy exclaimed loudly.

Alice saw Dan nod, bending down to exchange a few words with Charlie before the two of them walked to the car. Charlie was clearly keeping his distance from Dan.

'You're wet too, Alice!' Charlie looked her over. 'Not as wet as my dad…'

'I'm better at drying off than your dad is!' Alice joked and Charlie nodded, as if that went without saying.

'We'll drop Alice off and I'll tell you all about it when we get home, Charlie.' Dan opened the back door of the car and Charlie climbed into his seat, shrinking exaggeratedly when Dan leaned across to buckle him in.

CHAPTER NINE

ALICE HAD STOOD under a stream of warm, soapy water for a while, until the mud from the river had all disappeared from the shower tray. Today had been…

There were too many questions and not enough answers to go around. The thought of Dan as a child, alone and hungry, made her want to cry. And the thought of what he'd become, despite everything—that made her want to cry different tears.

But she knew now that he felt the thrill which sparked between them. They were both trying to ignore it but… Maybe she should be asking herself easier questions, but this was the only one she wanted an answer to at the moment.

It was nice to be clean and wearing dry clothes. Alice responded to a '*NON-URGENT*' message from Molly, giving Geeta's phone number, and then walked to Dan's house. Leaning on her stick at first, and then tucking it under her arm for the second half of the journey.

He didn't fail to notice, but Dan just smiled when she propped the stick up against the wall in the hallway. Alice was a little slower without it, but it was nice to feel that she could leave it behind if she wanted to.

'Where's Charlie?' The house was quiet, and Dan smelled…just wonderful. How did he do that—it was only soap?

'He's gone upstairs to make cards for Evan and Davey. I told him what had happened…in broad terms and emphasising the positive…and he decided that he wanted to send them both a card.'

'That's nice of him.'

Dan nodded, obviously pleased. 'He's a good kid. I told him to avoid any streams in his pictures. And especially people falling into them or lying on the ground. He's to concentrate on happy things.'

'Such as?' Alice reckoned that Charlie would probably have his own idea of what was a happy thing.

'Pizza. Or inter-galactic space travel. Both, maybe.'

'Sounds good. That would cheer me up. I got a text from Molly that Geeta had phoned the surgery and left a message for me. I called her back and she's heard from Elaine—the boys are both well but they're being kept in until tomorrow or Sunday for observation.'

Dan nodded. 'That's good to hear.'

'She's also considering doing a few sessions with kids and their parents—a fun afternoon for them with a serious message. She said she'd seen the posters at the surgery and the school, but she'd assumed that the river was a safe place for her kids, she's taught them all to swim and they paddle there all the time.'

'I think that's a big part of the problem. People think that cold water shock is something that's a hazard in the depths of winter. But running water can be cold enough even in the summer. What's Geeta thinking of doing—maybe the surgery should get involved?'

'I've already offered. I said I'd help her with some information sheets, and maybe we could find a few new places to display them. As soon as possible, since the summer holidays are when everyone's taking their kids out and there are a lot of lakes and streams around here.'

'You're ahead of me, then.' Dan smiled. 'You're okay with that?'

'Yes. I'll call her back tomorrow though, to discuss the details. This evening's for pizza and a little inter-galactic relaxation.' Alice bit her lip. The inter-galactic part was meant as a joke, but right now it felt as if she were on the brink of a new adventure. One that might involve exploring the unknown.

'We make a good team…' Dan murmured. Had

he stepped a little closer or had she? Maybe it was a case of faster-than-light personal travel.

'Yes. We do.' Both working independently of each other, but as one. Supporting each other, even though they'd only exchanged a few words and the odd glance.

She felt his fingers brush the back of her hand, his touch so feather-light that it would be easy to ignore. To walk into the kitchen and fetch the pizza delivery menu from the door of the fridge…

Alice reached out, touching his hand, and this time Dan curled his fingers around hers. So little, and yet so very much. Innocent, and yet with the bright thrill of the forbidden.

'I…' She reached up, caressing his cheek. 'I can't help this, Dan.'

'Nor can I.' They both knew that this was the wrong time and the wrong place. The wrong millennium, even. It was just stars in their eyes, which were too far away to reach, but somehow that didn't matter.

He was relaxed and gentle. Slow enough for her to pull away from him at any time. That just made it more compelling, more deliciously tantalising.

'Just one kiss…?' His eyes darkened as he spoke. It wasn't like Dan to be careless with words, but Alice knew that *just* wouldn't do it justice. And that *one* wouldn't be enough.

She reached up, curling her fingers around his neck. Waiting for a moment before she stood on her toes and brushed her lips against his. She heard Dan's sharp intake of breath, and then he kissed her.

It started off slow and tender, but neither of them could keep that up for long. She felt Dan's arm around her waist, pulling her against him. Felt his warmth leaking through the two layers of thin cotton between them. His strength, holding her tight.

Alice ran her hands across the sweet, tight curve of his shoulders. A little further, across the swell of his biceps, which hardened at her touch. She applied a little pressure and he responded, kissing her with a delicious hunger that recognised only the moment, and none of its consequences.

'Dad! What are you doing? Did you *ask* Alice if you could kiss her?'

The synchronicity was still working… Dan and Alice jumped apart at exactly the same moment. But Dan was a little slow in replying.

'Yes, Charlie. Your Dad asked me if I would like him to kiss me and I told him yes, I would. Thank you for checking.'

Charlie nodded, apparently satisfied with her answer. Alice wondered what his next question was going to be, and concentrated on not blushing.

'Because you always have to ask, don't you, Dad?'

'That's right. Well done, Charlie.' Dan had his

hands in his pockets now and was trying to look innocent, although that wasn't entirely working. Something about the slight twitch of his lips gave him the look of a delicious rogue.

'I've finished my cards. For Evan and Davey.'

'Have you?' Alice's smile was prompted by relief. 'May I see them?'

Charlie nodded, carrying his cards over to the sofa and sitting down. Alice sat next to him, looking over his shoulder. He'd decided to play it safe and go for giant flowers, growing past the roof of a small house.

'Is that your house?'

Charlie shook his head. 'No, it's your house. Your garden has sunflowers.'

'So it does. The cards are beautiful. I think that they'll really cheer Evan and Davey up.' Alice flipped open one of them, and saw that Dan had traced Charlie's name inside in pencil, and that Charlie had written over the letters in different-coloured crayons. 'I especially like this.'

'Nice job, Charlie.' Dan seemed to have regained the use of his limbs and had walked over to the sofa to peer at the cards. 'We'll find some envelopes and address them, and I'll take you to deliver them in the morning, before we go to the gym with Alice.'

Charlie nodded. 'Are we going to have pizza now, Dad?'

'Yes, I'll order it. You want ham and cheese?'

Charlie nodded in reply and Alice followed Dan into the kitchen to study the takeaway menu.

'*I'm pretty sure I asked. Although I didn't wait for an answer...*' he murmured quietly.

'*I don't think I left you in any doubt about my answer. You want to go and explain all that to Charlie?*' Alice whispered back, grinning up at him.

'*No, I... I think that's one of the things I'm going to leave until later to explain.*' Dan took her hand, squeezing it. '*Are we good?*'

'*You don't know?*' Alice looked behind her, in case Charlie had decided to follow them, before planting a kiss on his cheek. Dan nodded, the light returning to his eyes.

'What pizza do you want?'

'Cheese and pepperoni. Extra hot.'

Dan's hand strayed to his pocket and then he sighed. 'May I borrow your phone, please. Mine's drying out…hopefully.' He nodded towards a bowl of uncooked rice on the countertop.

Alice took her phone from her pocket and gave it to him. They'd kissed and it had been wonderful. Something she'd be mad not to want to repeat. That was why it was over now, because they both knew for sure that taking things any further would be special. The kind of special that was capable of altering lives…

They might be able to find a place for themselves. Somewhere that would meet Dan and

Charlie's needs as well as her own. But they both needed an absolute commitment and each of them had reasons to be wary of giving one.

One kiss, however spectacular, wasn't a commitment. They had a chance to go back, to take refuge on the safe ground of friendship. Alice would share pizza with Dan and Charlie and then go home, saying she needed an early night. And tomorrow this dragging regret, the feeling that she'd turned her back on something right, might ease.

It had been the kind of kiss that could knock a full-grown man off his feet. And Dan was getting over it.

He wasn't going to make excuses and pretend he'd been carried away in the moment, or that he'd made a mistake. Dan had wanted to kiss Alice, and he knew that she'd wanted to kiss him. They'd ignored all of the reasons they shouldn't get involved, two lives which had to diverge in order to thrive, and gone ahead. And now he had to get his head back into a place where Alice was his friend, and he could support her in leaving.

On Saturday, Dan had gone through the motions. He'd called for Alice and driven to the gym, helping her exercise while Charlie played in the children's soft play area. When that intimacy was too much to bear, Dan had hit the treadmill and run himself into a place where he could accept the decisions they'd made. He and Charlie had helped her buy a dress and then gone for lunch. He'd watched Charlie hug his goodbye, when Dan could only offer a, '*See you later.*'

And then the hurt had begun to lift. Alice had spent Sunday with Geeta, discussing their plans for a low-key campaign to make sure that parents in the village knew of the risks involved in their children playing near water, and Dan and Charlie had spent the afternoon watching a double-feature at the cinema. A new week brought new challenges, and soon they were back on course.

'How are they?' Dan had been to visit Evan and Davey at home on Thursday afternoon, and returned to find Alice had stayed back at the surgery, waiting for news.

'They're both well, physically. Elaine told me that Evan's been having nightmares, though.' Dan unlocked the door of his consulting room, motioning Alice inside.

'He seemed to know what was going on a great deal better than Davey. Maybe he remembers too much.' Alice sat down.

'Yes, that could well be the case. Although we can't be entirely sure how much either of the boys remembers. John McIntyre is an accredited counsellor, and Elaine's agreed to bring the boys in to see him so that they can talk about their experiences. We'll go from there. It's a tough thing for anyone to go through, the initial shock to the body is immense.'

'It's something I don't see a lot of. How people recover from the trauma of injury.' Alice turned the corners of her mouth down. 'Although I've had some personal experience of it lately.'

'Everyone's different, even two brothers, hurt in the same accident. Elaine's already letting each of them take things at their own pace and in their own way. I think that's going to help a lot.'

'Then we'll…' Alice corrected herself. It was likely that the careful process of allowing each of the boys to come to terms with their experience would take longer than the few weeks she'd be spending here. '*You'll* be keeping an eye on them.'

'Yes. You saw Jasmine this afternoon, didn't you? How's she doing?'

'Well. I told her that I'd left my stick behind last week.'

Dan chuckled. The only way that Alice ever met a challenge was head-on. 'And how did that go?'

'We laughed about it. I think she's in on the secret that we doctors try to hide—that just because we *are* doctors we're not immune to making every single patient-mistake in the book.'

'Not every single one, surely? And at least we know we're making them.'

'Doesn't that make it worse? Being perfectly

aware that you're making a mistake but still making it.'

'Yeah. Maybe. I'll defer to your judgement in that respect.' Dan held his hands up in a gesture of surrender. 'So, have you thought any more about tomorrow evening, and Molly's party?'

Alice raised her eyebrows. 'I thought I was supposed to be forgetting all about that until the very last minute.'

'Charlie asked me to ask you. He says he won't see you for a whole two weeks, which is quite a long time if you're only five.' Dan's parents would be coming to pick Charlie up on Saturday, and he'd be staying with them in London for the next fortnight.

'Long time for you as well?' Alice asked.

'I wasn't going to admit to that. When he went to stay with them last summer they all had a marvellous time. Their to-do list for this year seems to be growing by the day.'

'Well, maybe you need a to-do list as well. Drive to Cambridge and… I don't know, do something touristy?'

Dan shrugged. 'Actually, I was thinking of alternating between sulking and worrying.'

'Try that when I'm around and I'll think of something for you to do. And since Charlie's asked, yes, I will come tomorrow evening. I might spend most of my time with the kids in the pub garden and then leave early, but I'll be there.'

'Do whatever you feel most comfortable with. Charlie will be very pleased to hear that you're coming.' So was Dan, but he probably shouldn't mention that. 'I'll pick you up at seven?'

'Yes. Seven's good…' Just three words from Alice were enough to make Dan happier than he had any right to be.

CHAPTER TEN

DAN HAD ALREADY seen the emerald-green dress that shimmered with all of the colours of a peacock's tail. But he hadn't seen Alice actually wearing it, and that made all of the difference in the world.

'You look beautiful!' Charlie declared, and Dan wondered what he was going to do for the next fortnight, with no one to hug Alice or tell her she looked beautiful on his behalf. Perhaps he'd just have to do it himself.

'And you look very handsome.' Alice bent down, straightening the open collar of Charlie's red and brown checked shirt and giving Dan a sidelong smile. 'Both of you.'

When they got to the Swan Inn, the quiet country pub seemed to be host to at least half of the village, along with a large number of people from the surrounding area. Dan slid into the last space in the car park and they headed straight for the large garden, where a brightly coloured tent had been pitched. Several women were supervising the children, who had their own food and drinks table, which was clearly the territory of one of Molly's daughters, who was helping the children fill their plates.

'Hello Charlie…' Geeta emerged from the melee, dressed in red and smiling down at the boy. Then she turned to Dan and Alice. 'So nice to see you both. You look wonderful, Alice.'

'So do you! What a good idea to have a tent for the children, it keeps them all in one place. Are you going to be out here all evening?' Alice replied, looking around.

'I prefer it actually. It's a bit crowded inside the pub, it's much nicer out here.'

Alice nodded. 'I don't suppose I could stay for a while, could I? Those mini pizzas look nice…' She gestured towards the food table.

She was chickening out. Fair enough, Dan had told her that whatever she wanted to do when they arrived was okay, but he felt an unwelcome stab of disappointment that Alice didn't seem disposed to even try to face the party inside.

But Geeta came to the rescue. 'Oh, no, you don't, that food is strictly for the under-tens. And you have to at least go and say hello to Molly.' She took Charlie's hand. 'Would you like some pizza, Charlie?'

'See you later, Dad.' Charlie had clearly decided that he and Alice belonged elsewhere as well, and followed Geeta across to the table to collect a paper plate and choose what he wanted to eat.

Alice puffed out a sigh. 'Seems we can't crash this party, then.'

She turned towards the back door of the pub, seeming to stumble a little as she did so. She had left her stick in the car, and Dan felt her fingers on his arm, reaching for support. He tucked her hand into the crook of his elbow in a silent signal that whatever they did now, they'd do together.

And then his moment came. Alice walked into the pub on his arm, their bodies close as she hung on to him for support. The chatter of voices somehow didn't fall quiet on their entrance, which was strange considering how gorgeous Alice looked, but probably just as well since she was obviously very nervous.

Molly was busy working the room, but when she caught sight of them she made a beeline for Alice. 'I'm so glad you could make it!' Molly enveloped Alice in an excited hug.

'You look fabulous.' Alice smiled suddenly. 'I didn't realise that *come-as-you-are* allowed for sequins.'

Molly ran her fingers over the sequinned bodice of her black dress. 'Come as you are could mean anything, couldn't it? Since I've turned fifty now, I think it's permissible to wear sequins to the supermarket if it takes my fancy. What do you think?'

'Sounds like an excellent plan. Along with a feather boa, I hope.'

'Oh, of course. Now, you see those balloons in the corner?'

'They're difficult to miss.' Dan looked across at the balloons, which were spread across the ceiling in a riot of colour. 'Can I take a wild guess that there are fifty of them?'

'We counted them three times and there *were* forty-nine. That's not quite the same, is it, so I added another one. But *below* the balloons my husband's busy pouring glasses of wine, and there's some alcohol-free punch which is rather tasty even though I say it myself. There's plenty of food and the bar's open in case you want anything different to drink.'

Molly glanced over her shoulder. 'Oh, my life, there's Mrs Grimshaw from the bridge club. I asked them all but I didn't think she'd be coming, I'd better go and find her somewhere to sit…'

'I didn't know that Molly played bridge,' Alice murmured as Molly hurried away to take the arm of one of the village's oldest inhabitants and guide her to a seat.

'Molly tried out practically every club in the village when her youngest daughter left home for university. She settled on embroidery because it was calming, and bridge because she liked the cut and thrust of it all. Patrick told me that she's a very good player.'

'Really? When I lived here, Molly used to be rushing home every evening to cook dinner. I suppose life moves on…'

Dan nodded, wondering what he'd be doing when Charlie decided to fly the nest. He didn't need to think about that just yet. 'Would you like a drink?'

'I'll try the punch, I think.' Alice scanned the room, clearly wondering what to do with herself while Dan braved the crowd around the drinks table. 'Oh, look. There are Jasmine's parents…'

Jasmine's mother was waving and beckoning to Alice to join them at their table. Dan sent her a silent thank-you and walked with her over to the couple, leaving Alice to be introduced to Jasmine's father while he got the drinks.

John McIntyre arrived just in time to sing '*Happy Birthday*' and eat a piece of cake, joking that if Molly could be persuaded to hold a party every Friday then Dan would have to think about cancelling Friday evening surgeries, as he'd dawdled through the list of patients for this evening in less than an hour. Dan was just beginning to let his guard down when a couple he didn't know buttonholed Alice.

'You're Dr Allenby's girl, aren't you?' The man had an air of having tracked down his prey.

Alice flushed red, her smile draining from her face. 'Yes, Alice Allenby. Mr and Mrs Pettifer?'

'That's right.' The woman smiled. 'I'm surprised you even recognise us; we moved to London some time ago. We're here visiting our son, and he said that we absolutely must come along to the party, we were sure to come across a few faces we knew.'

If this was a reunion, it clearly wasn't a happy one. Not from Alice's point of view, at least. 'It's nice to see you again, after all this time.' Her manner was courteous in the extreme, but the golden light had died in her eyes.

'We had to move…' Mr Pettifer seemed quite at ease with the situation. 'My company was growing fast, and London has a completely different scale of business opportunities.'

'We've been doing very well,' Mrs Pettifer added.

Something was up. Alice wasn't responding to their smiles, but she appeared determined to stand her ground. Dan leaned forward, holding out his hand.

'Dan Ryan. I'm the local GP…'

'Ah, yes.' Mr Pettifer shook his hand. 'We heard that Patrick Allenby died recently. Such a shame that you were estranged, Alice.' His manner seemed almost confrontational.

'My father and I were always close.' There was an edge of outrage to Alice's tone.

'Is that Charlie's cake?' Dan asked her, pointing to the paper plate in her hand. 'We'd better take it to him…'

Alice seemed to be considering the opportunity for escape he was offering. Then he saw her back stiffen. 'No, it's mine. Molly's daughter came to collect some for the children's tent.'

Okay. If that was the way she wanted it. But Dan wasn't moving from her side now.

'That silly business after the accident…' It was quite clear that Mr Pettifer hadn't finished with his jaunt down memory lane. 'I don't think you really understood at the time, Alice. The lad's parents were devastated, and there was nothing that anyone could say to console them.'

'Of course not,' Alice agreed. Dan saw her hand begin to shake, and he quietly took the plate she was holding and put it down on a nearby table.

Mrs Pettifer nodded, seeming quite oblivious to Alice's distress. 'And when they found out about the drugs. What else were they supposed to think?'

'I'm sorry…' Dan wasn't sorry at all, but this conversation already reeked of insincerity. 'What *did* they think?'

'Well, it occurred to his mother that Alice might have supplied them. We all found out differently, of course, but it wouldn't have been very tactful for my wife to disagree with her.' Mr Pettifer clearly reckoned that he was an authority on tact. Along with everything else, perhaps. 'It was an honest mistake, and it really wasn't necessary to leave the village like that. Don't you see that now, Alice?'

Was this an apology? Maybe an insincere one, which sought only to justify their cruelty and make the couple feel better about themselves. Which Dan didn't really class as an apology at all.

Alice didn't reply. But something told Dan that she wasn't going to back down and agree with them. This meant too much to her, and the suggestion that she and Patrick had been estranged had clearly hurt.

'What I see is that a nineteen-year-old who'd been through a traumatic experience was treated unfairly. You do realise that accusing her of supplying drugs might well have destroyed Alice's hopes of pursuing a career as a doctor, don't you?'

'Well, for all we knew she may have done.' Mrs Pettifer shot Dan an outraged look. 'The boy's parents certainly didn't know about any drug use on his part…'

'Sadly, parents are often the last to know. It must have come as a terrible shock to them, but that's no justification for spreading rumours and making unjustified accusations which could have resulted in Alice being prosecuted. Or for insinuating that Patrick Allenby had anything other than complete faith in his daughter, and maintained a close relationship with her. The latter is something I *do* know about, and witnessed first-hand.'

Maybe he'd gone a little too far. But Alice's hand had found its way to his arm and her fingers were doing the talking for her. Unless he was very much mistaken, that gentle squeeze was one of approbation.

'Well.' Mr Pettifer frowned at him. 'I'm sorry you see it like that.'

Suddenly Alice spoke up. 'I'm sorry that you don't. I'm afraid we're going to have to agree to differ.'

That was generous of her. But Mr Pettifer rejected the gift, turning away from them. His wife followed him without so much as a backward glance and Dan heard his own sigh of relief.

'Can we run now? Please…' Alice looked up at him.

'Yeah. I was just going to suggest that.'

They escaped the noise and laughter of the pub and Dan found a secluded bench in the garden where they could sit. Alice was silent, lost in her own thoughts.

'Would you like me to go and get Charlie? We can go back to mine…' he asked, wondering what he could do or say to comfort her.

'It's not necessary. Don't drag Charlie away from *his* party.' Alice gave him a tight smile.

Fair enough. Alice wasn't so much running,

just stepping back to regroup. 'What they said, Alice…'

'I know. Graham Pettifer never did much like being in the wrong—Dad used to say that he had to go to London in order to expand his company because there weren't enough people here who were prepared to work for him. And Jan Pettifer was the one who was behind all of the rumours.'

'Not the parents?'

Alice shrugged. 'I expect they said it; they were in shock and understandably wanting to think the best of their son. One thing that Graham Pettifer said was right. You can't attach any blame to them.'

'I doubt he meant it in quite the way you do. He doesn't strike me as a particularly understanding or generous man.'

'No. He never struck me as that either.' Alice turned to him. 'Thanks for what you said, Dan. I really appreciate it.'

'It's only the truth. I'm glad you persuaded me to come to the party.'

'Wait… *I* persuaded *you*? I thought you'd persuaded me!'

Suddenly the quiet existence of a country doctor with a young child seemed just that. An existence, not a life. Something that Dan had done to ensure Charlie's future rather than his own.

'I generally show my face at this kind of thing and then make an excuse to leave. Being a doctor *and* a parent gives me plenty of excuses. And when I first came here Charlie was just a baby, so it's not as if I have a track-record of going out all that much.'

Alice nodded, smiling. 'Village expectations, eh? No one forgets how you once were. It makes change a little more difficult.'

And Dan *had* changed, almost without knowing it. He'd come here a wounded man, grieving for his wife and afraid of even entertaining the idea that he might move on in the future, in case he was left alone again. He'd never forget Nola, but Alice had given him a future back, however hard and uncertain it seemed.

'I'm not so sure about that. Maybe the expectations just make the changes more difficult to notice? But things *do* change.' Dan stretched his arm along the back-rest of the bench behind Alice. Not touching her, but there was always the possibility that he might.

'Do you mean that?' Alice turned towards him, her eyes blazing in the last rays of evening sunshine that stretched across the grass towards them.

Dan thought for a moment. When the Pettifers had wounded Alice, they'd wounded him too. He couldn't separate her happiness from his, they were one and the same. Dan wasn't sure yet, no one could be after just two weeks, but what he and Alice had might just be real.

'Yeah.' He retrieved her hand from her lap, raising it to his lips to brush a kiss against her fingers. 'I mean it.'

Everything had changed. Apart from Graham and Jan Pettifer, of course, but that would be a bit too much to ask. But when Dan had spoken up for her he'd made Alice believe that she wasn't at fault. And she'd made the discovery that once you believed in yourself, what other people thought didn't matter so much.

The evening was still warm, and they watched as the Pettifers walked across the car park, talking rapidly to each other. Right now, Alice didn't much care what they were saying, just that they were leaving. They got into a large red car that was parked across the back of several others, including Dan's.

'So they're the ones who blocked us in.' Dan chuckled. He'd relaxed now, his arm almost touching her back. One inch away from an embrace.

Not yet. Not while the highs and lows of this evening were still fresh in both of their hearts. It was enough to know that nothing was set in stone between them anymore.

'Just as well we didn't decide to run too far. What would have happened if Charlie was ready to go? You'd never have got past them.'

'Charlie's okay.' Dan took his new phone from

his pocket, purchased after he'd finally admitted that the old one hadn't benefitted too much from being submerged in rice. 'They're reading a story, and Amy's gone to sleep…'

Alice leaned across, looking at the series of texts which updated parents on what was going on in the tent and who wanted to go home. 'Geeta's very organised.'

'*Very.* It's reassuring, though. I could concentrate on the Pettifers without wondering whether Charlie was getting into mischief while my back was turned.' He nodded towards a couple who were making their way from the back door of the pub, towards the tent. 'There are Amy's parents. Right on cue.'

'I didn't realise…' Alice felt a stab of guilt. She'd been enjoying the party—and then *not* enjoying it—without even thinking what Charlie might be up to. 'It's a full-time job, isn't it.'

'Yeah. Charlie's always my first concern.' Dan caught her gaze. 'He doesn't have to be my *only* concern, though.'

A little shiver ran down Alice's spine. Were they working something out, here? 'I wouldn't like you so much if Charlie didn't come first.'

He nodded, smiling. 'Shall we go and say our goodbyes? By the time we've worked our way around everyone, Charlie probably *will* be ready to doze off. Or do you want to stay? Geeta will be settling the kids down after they've finished the story.'

'Let Charlie sleep in his own bed. And I'm ready for goodbyes.' Alice would say goodbye to Dan tonight—they too needed to sleep in their own beds before they made any rash promises. But who knew what tomorrow might bring…?

CHAPTER ELEVEN

ALICE HAD WISHED Charlie a happy holiday with his grandparents and given him an extra-big hug last night. There was no reason to pop round to Dan's place to see him again this morning, but all the same she woke early and had to stop herself from rushing to the shower and missing breakfast before setting out.

Dan had said that his parents would be arriving around ten, and aimed to get back to London in time for lunch. She left home at eleven, reckoning that would give Dan time to say his goodbyes to Charlie then sit down and collect his thoughts. Alice hoped he'd be relaxed and yet capable of seeing everything in perspective today. Whatever that perspective might reveal.

As she approached his house she saw a car turn out of the driveway. Clearly, she'd miscalculated but she was too eager to see Dan to turn back now. When she turned into Dan's driveway, he was leaning in his front doorway.

'Was that your parents I saw? I thought they were coming to collect Charlie at ten?'

Dan nodded. 'They did. Charlie's been up since five this morning, changing his mind about what he wants to take with him.'

'Oh. Was that a way of telling you that he didn't want to go?'

Dan took one last, lingering look in the direction that the car had taken, down to the village. Then he turned his gaze onto her, suddenly present and in this moment, and beckoned her inside.

'I think it was a way of telling me that he was quite happy to move out until Christmas as long as I gave him a call every now and then and alert Santa to his change of address. He has a great time with my parents and since it's his holiday it's only right that they spoil him a bit.'

Alice wasn't quite sure how to respond to that. 'I'm sure he's going to miss you, though.'

'He'll get around to it. But he's five and right now he's going on an amazing adventure with two people that he loves. I'm just happy I managed to dissuade him from taking his winter coat—my parents' car is roomy but there are limits.'

'You seem pretty okay with it all.'

Dan smiled. 'This is like his first day of school on steroids. I made it to the surgery, and then Molly brought me a cup of coffee and some of the nice biscuits she keeps for emergencies, and told me that when I went to pick him up that afternoon he'd be all smiles and telling me about his amazing day. I managed to hold it together until she was out of the room, and then I shed a tear. Or two.'

'And this is two weeks…'

'Yeah. Would you think any less of me if I curled up in a corner and wailed for a while?'

'Be my guest.' This was far more the Dan that she knew. Always there for Charlie and trying to do his best for him. 'Getting it out in the open will always make a person feel better.'

'I expect so. Coffee?'

'Yes. No biscuits, I had an enormous breakfast.'

'Okay. I'm having some toast. I didn't dare go into the kitchen to grab anything to eat in case Charlie tried to put his bed into his suitcase… Do you have some spare time today? I was wondering if you might like to go to the garden centre after we've hit the supermarket.'

'You're thinking of planting something?'

'Maybe we could look at some trees, for the surgery garden? For Patrick. We talked about it a while ago and if you'd still like to do that…does the time seem right now?'

In all that had happened in the last two weeks, Alice had put her father's memorial to the back of her mind. But now the time *did* seem right. She could plant trees and believe in a future where the rain and the sun would nourish them and make them grow.

'I'd really like that. And now's the time for it.'

Dan nodded. 'I think so. You're sure you don't want any toast...?'

Alice had to return nearly half the fruit and vegetables in Dan's trolley back to the shelves, since he'd be cooking for one for the next couple of weeks. But when they'd paid for their shopping, leaving it in cool bags in the boot of his car, and driven on to the garden centre, he seemed more animated.

They walked past lines of trees of all different kinds, carefully studying their growing requirements and final height.

'I was thinking not too tall. What do you reckon?' Dan offered his opinion.

'Probably. Not too small, though.'

'Yeah, definitely not too small...' He looked around. 'There's a lot here.'

'Maybe if we made a list and ticked things off one by one. If there were just five or six to choose from it would be much easier.' Alice was beginning to feel that nothing she'd seen was entirely right. Or entirely wrong, for that matter.

'Yeah.' Dan thought for a moment and then shook his head. 'No. Why don't we go for the impractical option?'

'Really? Tell me more, I'm not following your logic yet.'

'You know how Patrick always used to say that if you're not sure what to do next, just close your eyes and do what feels right?'

'Yes…?'

'Why don't we stop looking at trees here, and go and sit on the grass at the surgery and eat pizza? Close our eyes and do what feels right.'

'But it's not Friday.' Alice knew that Charlie would eat pizza every night of the week if he could, and that Dan had imposed an only-on-Fridays rule. 'The other part sounds like a good possibility.'

'Did *you* have pizza last night?'

'Well…no.'

'Neither did I. I think Charlie did, and no doubt he'll be trying to convince my parents that rules don't apply when you're on holiday, but we'll leave that to them. We could pick up a pizza on our way home, drop the shopping before your ice cream melts, and then go to the surgery…'

'No. Definitely not, Dan. We'll drop the shopping, take the ice cream with us and put it into the freezer compartment at the surgery and then have the pizza delivered—this is far too important a decision to make on cold pizza. Then we can sit on the grass and eat ice cream. And do what feels right.'

Dan nodded. 'That sounds much better…'

* * *

Alice's practicality had transformed the impractical into something that would work but still left some room for the imagination. They'd sat down on the grass in the garden at the surgery and shared a large, piping-hot pizza. Then ice cream. And then Alice had flopped onto her back, staring at the sky, and Dan had followed suit.

'I could just…a little dappled shade would be nice, right now.' She closed her eyes. 'Something I could feel as well as see.'

'With you all the way.'

'Something to change with the seasons and… Silver birch! Dad always liked silver birch.'

Dan chuckled. 'Yeah. Good decision. One of the smaller varieties?'

'Yes, definitely. And which of the benches did you like the best? I rather liked the one we sat in for a while. It was comfortable and not too fussy.'

'Yes, I agree. Did you want a brass plate for the back, with Patrick's name on it?'

'No. How about having Dad's initials carved into the wood somewhere? So that he's there and remembered, but it's a bit more organic,' Alice suggested.

'Much better.'

They fell silent, lying on the grass in the sunshine. This was nice… Companionable.

No. No, it wasn't companionable. It felt like making love, without the physical contact. Although touching Dan would definitely make it a great deal better.

'Did you mean it, Dan? What you said last night?'

He laughed. 'I meant everything I said last night. Are you going to give me a clue which bit you're currently referring to?'

'About changing. That you felt you'd changed since you came here.'

'Yes, I do. When Nola died, and for a long time afterwards, I felt that the best I could hope for was a measure of peace. But I think that moving on has become an option now.'

'So you're reckoning on putting yourself back on the market?' Alice turned the corners of her mouth down. It was difficult to sound non-committal without veering sharply into the impersonal.

She heard him move and opened her eyes, sitting up. Dan was propped on one elbow, regarding her thoughtfully. 'Only very limited availability.' He held up one finger.

'Just one? Mine's a very strictly curated list, too.' She brushed one of her fingers against his.

'It's a risk.'

'I know.' They didn't need to reiterate all of the things that could go wrong. And if things went right then there was a whole new set of roadblocks to contend with.

'We could end up hurting each other. Very probably will.'

'But maybe we won't. And I'm hurting already, Dan.'

Warmth bloomed in his eyes. 'Anything I can do for that?'

'Take me home, and I'll tell you exactly what you can do for it.'

Dan got to his feet, offering her his arm. He'd done that a hundred times before and Alice had taken it, but this time was different. They walked back through the open French windows of the consulting room that Alice had been using for the last two weeks and Dan stopped to kiss her.

He stopped again when they reached the front door of the surgery, for another kiss. This time it was warmer and just a little wilder. 'We're taking it slow, then?' Alice smiled up at him.

'Too risky?' Clearly Dan's definition of slow didn't mean careful—at least not in this context. It was a long, languid exploration that went way past the immediate need to satisfy each other.

'I don't care, Dan. I want to take those risks with you. We'll be there for each other.'

'You can count on it.' He kissed her again, and then unlocked the front door of the surgery.

This was against all of the odds. A woman as gorgeous as Alice who wanted him perhaps almost as much as he wanted her. They connected on every level, as friends, co-workers and now… Dan knew that they could connect as lovers. The only question was whether he could survive the sweet, slow pace that Alice seemed to want as much as he did.

He was going to have to. Because he wasn't missing a moment of it. Even driving back to his house and walking steadily towards the front door, with her holding onto his arm, was exquisite. Tantalising shadows in the brilliance of what might come next.

When the front door clicked shut behind them there was no dash for either the stairs or the sofa, but another kiss. She pressed herself against him and Dan turned her around, her back against the door. She must be able to feel his arousal now, and her gasp told him that it was exactly what Alice wanted.

'Any moment now… I'm going to have to sweep you off your feet and take you upstairs.'

'Oh, no, you're not, Dan.' He'd forgotten to add straight-talking to the list of things he loved about Alice. 'You showed me how to stand on my own two feet. Don't let me down now.'

'You can manage them?' The stairs in Patrick's older house were a little steeper, but they had the advantage of being narrower, so that Alice could hold onto the bannisters on both sides.

'I've been practising stairs at the gym. I can do it.'

Dan took the precaution of walking up with her, and she didn't wobble once. She waved him away as she walked along the upstairs hallway, but when they reached the bedroom, she was all his. It felt like an achievement they'd made together. One that matched the change in his own life, and his realisation that he was finally able to reach out to someone.

And now he was confident in his own skin, which Alice seemed to like so much. In the idea that a future for them wasn't impossible, even though neither of them knew what that future might look like.

It had been delicious. Stretched out on Dan's bed, her knee propped on a pillow that he'd carefully positioned beneath her knee to support it. If Alice had learned only one thing, she'd learned it well. Dan knew exactly what to do with a woman's body.

At first, it had been slow and leisurely. An appreciation. An exploration. And then came the risk. Would they go too far and end it all too soon? Not far enough, and find that the carefully cultivated passion had waned? But then came the reward. Both of them so lost in pleasure, so aware of each other that every touch was exquisite.

Her final climax came along with his, roaring through them both like a hurricane. And then there was quiet, just the sound of Dan's laboured breathing and hers. The feel of his skin, and the scent of lovemaking.

'You think we did that right?' Alice was sprawled on top of him, barely able to move.

Dan chuckled. 'You really have to ask?'

'No. I just wanted to hear you say it.'

'I don't have the words for what we just did.' His fingers caressed her cheek, leaving echoes of sensation behind them. 'But yes. We did it right.'

CHAPTER TWELVE

THE WEEKEND HAD been one long sigh of relief. As if the grief, pain and uncertainty had been driven out of her, allowing Alice to finally relax. Dan was different, too. Less guarded, more playful. And the blue-eyed smile that she loved so much seemed more boyish.

On Sunday afternoon Dan brought a wide hammock from the garage, stringing it up between two old trees at the end of the garden. There was no need to dress up for it, Dan was bare-chested still and wearing a pair of casual shorts and one of his T-shirts would do for Alice in the secluded garden. They lay in the dappled shade, enjoying the breeze of a summer's afternoon. Together, still.

'I have to drop in to see Geeta at around four o'clock. We've decided how to approach our information drive about cold water shock.'

'Yeah? Maybe I'll catch up on some paperwork while I'm waiting for you to get back.' Dan's fingers strayed to her shoulder, in one of those caresses that were now a part of the everyday. 'You and Geeta have a plan?'

'I think so. I've been calling a few people during the week and...' Alice and Geeta's plan had run away with itself and become something bigger and better. All that remained was to get Dan on board. 'I meant to ask you about this yesterday, but it slipped my mind.' She snuggled against him, kissing his cheek. They'd been far too occupied with each other.

'Glad to hear that. I wouldn't want to think that your attention's been straying...' He shifted closer and the hammock began to sway slightly. 'Ever made love in a hammock?'

'No! And I need to discuss this with you, Dan. Now!' Curiosity got the better of her. 'Have you?'

'No.' He gave her a dangerous smile. 'Maybe we'll save that for next weekend? What's yours and Geeta's plan?'

Alice was thinking about next weekend, now. They'd been so immersed in the here-and-now that the future had been irrelevant, but now that Dan had spoken about it, she wanted next weekend more than anything.

Concentrate! Think about something other than the soft sway of a hammock and the summer breeze...

'I've been calling a few people.' Her voice sounded surprisingly businesslike. 'Reverend Foster and Tabatha Green.'

'You want to get the church and the local paper involved?'

'We're considering a monthly newsletter. Something like *Health Hints for September...*' Alice wrinkled her nose. 'That's not very snappy, but I'm sure that Tabatha could think of something better. Rev Foster says that we can have some space on the information board in the lobby of the church hall—people are in and out of there all the time. And Tabatha said we could have a monthly spot in the paper for free, it's just the kind of thing she's looking for as part of their commitment to community issues.'

Dan thought for a moment. 'It's a good idea. Patrick and I were thinking that we needed to reorganise all the information leaflets in the waiting room at the surgery—some of them have been there for ages and I'm not sure that anyone reads them. I've been meaning to do it but haven't had the time.'

'But things are starting to ease a bit now. And we've started the legal arrangements for transferring my shares in the practice to you, so you'll be able to think about getting someone permanent in, which will take a lot of the pressure off in the long run. I could do the first few newsletters and then perhaps you could take over. Maybe not write them all but get someone else to do it. That might work really well, allow people to feel that they know everyone in the practice.'

He was still, suddenly. Silent. Alice could practically see the thoughts turning in his head.

'You're not going to stay, are you?'

The first thing that Alice had thought of when she'd woken up this morning was what it would be like to do this every day. And then *this* day had taken over and carried her forward on its sweet momentum.

'Dan, I... This is all so new. We promised each other that we'd be there to see where it led us but...'

He nodded. 'That doesn't mean you'll actually be *here*.'

'It doesn't mean that you'll be upping sticks and coming with me when I go back to work either.' Their relationship had been fragile from the start. Risky. But if this was where they broke, then it was too soon.

'You're right. I'm sorry.'

Alice could almost breathe again. Almost... Somewhere, off in the distance, she could hear a clamour of voices from the past, which had formed up with military precision and were marching on their future together.

Then Dan spoke. 'I know it's far too early but...can we make a plan?'

He was fighting back. But stark, on the horizon, the approaching army was standing its ground. Banners floating in the breeze and ready to attack.

'I think we should. If a plan is what we both need, then it's not too early for us.'

He nodded. 'I could drive down to see you every other weekend. Drop Charlie off with Mum and Dad if the three of them have something planned, or maybe bring him with me.'

'I'd like it if you brought him. I've a spare room that Dad used to use, and Charlie could make it his own.'

Dan grinned, nodding. 'I'd like that too—although Charlie's ever-growing social schedule might mean he can't make it every time.'

'We can be flexible; it's a three-way arrangement. And I'd come to see you every other weekend, too. We can fit together like...' Alice smiled. Like lovers. They knew how to do that, now.

Dan was clearly thinking the same and the hammock swayed as he folded her into an embrace, his body different from hers, but that just meant that there were no gaps in their armour.

'I'd love it if you would. And flexible's good. If you have something else to do at the weekend, I'll cultivate the art of missing you.'

'I might just cultivate the art of carrying on with my life. Allowing the village to be a part of it, but not everything.'

Dan nodded. 'Yeah, that would be good, too.'

Somewhere on the horizon, the forces that had gathered against them were beginning to disband. Running for cover. They weren't gone, but today's battle had been won. And when Dan kissed her, the sweet immediacy of the here and now didn't allow Alice to see anything else.

His hand plucked at the hem of her T-shirt. 'It's two hours before you have to be at Geeta's…'

It was tempting. 'But I have to go home and change my clothes…'

'I'll give you a lift home and then on to Geeta's…' Dan caught his breath as Alice moved his hand onto her breast.

'Then we could leave at a quarter past three…' Alice gasped as his fingers began to caress the thin cotton that separated them. The sweet shock of having him pull the T-shirt over her head and throw it to one side was still to come. But it *was* coming, and it made the here and now all the more delicious.

'I guess an hour and a quarter's enough…'

Sheer pleasure began to flood through her. Words didn't get any more arousing than this. 'Enough for what?'

'Let's find out.'

The future that had suddenly opened up ahead of them made it even more exquisitely exciting. This time Dan *did* carry her up the stairs. It was only practical; they were both in a hurry. He stripped off her T-shirt in one smooth movement, laying her down on the bed before taking off his shorts and reaching for the condoms.

'Dan…?' This was something new. An urgency that she hadn't felt before.

'Are you ready?'

'You need to ask?' She grinned at him. His hand slipped between her legs and Alice struggled to breathe.

'No, I don't…'

All the same, he made sure, letting her feel what would come next. Alice couldn't wait any longer, grabbing the condom from where he'd left it on the pillow beside them and rolling it down in place. Touching, caressing, giving him no choice…

They'd both gone from zero to everything in less time than it would have taken a kettle to boil. Alice could feel the first murmurs of a climax, and just as she began to give herself up to it, she heard Dan cry out. Felt his body stiffen as he rode the wave of his own pleasure.

'Sorry… Sorry.' He was still now, sweat on his brow. Alice pulled him down into her arms.

'Don't be. You've already shown me how you can wait for me. I love it that you couldn't this time.'

He shook his head, lifting his weight from her. Kissing her and then rolling her onto her side and curling his body around her back. 'All the same… it's not right.'

'Don't you want to rest?' Her body was still

buzzing with desire and Alice was hoping for a *no*.

'And miss what happens next?' He slid his arms around her, one hand on her breast, the other travelling downwards. Alice jolted against him as he kissed her neck, whispering what *was* going to happen next.

It was all the sweeter because he'd already given himself to her. Knowing how much he'd wanted her was powerful magic, and maybe it was time to let the last of her inhibitions go now, and show Dan just how much she could want him.

Maybe he'd been right. Dan never would love another woman the way he'd loved Nola. He'd never feel the same things with anyone else. He'd missed the most important point, though. Love was just one word, one feeling, but its most intriguing characteristic was that it was different every time. Loving Alice didn't replace his love for Nola, just as loving Charlie didn't replace his love for his parents.

Being able to share his work with Alice and discussing the ups and downs of their respective days over a mug of tea or a glass of wine before dinner was a new pleasure. One that they'd stretched to its very limit at first, since Charlie wasn't around to divert Dan's attention. But they'd laughingly come to the conclusion that as soon as the dinner plates hit the table the shop talk stopped.

'John mentioned that he'd had his first session with Evan and Davey yesterday. He said it went really well.'

Alice nodded. 'He spoke to the whole family together?'

'Yes, for starters. He says he may see both boys separately next time, he'll see what Elaine thinks. Davey's getting on well, but Evan was more aware of what was happening and feels guilty over encouraging his younger brother to jump into the water.'

'Is he sleeping any better?' Alice knew that Evan had been having night terrors.

'It's early days, but Elaine called John today and said that Evan slept through the night last night. He says he has a way to go with them still, but he's very optimistic. How's the newsletter doing?'

'I finished it today. Geeta spoke to Elaine, we wanted to see how she felt about us writing about cold water shock, and she was all in favour of it. She even asked Geeta if we could include a couple of quotes from her. I emailed it through to Tabatha—she wants to publish in the paper first, before we put it on the various noticeboards around the village—and she said it had *zing*.' Alice smirked at him, clearly liking the idea.

Dan liked it too. 'Nice one. That's just what we

need. I saw Kayla Matthews in the waiting room, she seemed a lot better.'

'Yes, she is. The tiredness and muscle pains turned out to be a low-grade infection and the antibiotics are working well.'

'That was a good spot.' Dan had been wondering what the practice would do without Alice, and dreading the procession of temporary doctors who would replace her, but he'd been saving the good news until last.

'John's told me that he's willing to stay on after you leave. Four days a week.'

'Really?' Alice clinked her glass against his. 'That's really good news, particularly since four days of John's help is generally worth five of anyone else's.' She frowned suddenly. 'Dad said he was so keen to retire, though…'

'I asked what brought on this sudden change of heart. He says that he doesn't regret the move that he and Adele made, to be closer to their daughter, but since Adele has another year to go before she retires and their daughter works too, he's been finding himself at a loose end during the day. He also confessed to having missed working with patients. His old job was largely red-tape and paperwork.'

Alice nodded. 'Yes, Dad told me that he'd said he thought he was losing touch with why he became a doctor in the first place. I assume you said yes—how long is he planning to stay?'

'For another year, until Adele retires. Then they'll go off island-hopping or whatever it is retirees do these days. But that gives me plenty of time to find someone who's a really good fit for the practice, to replace him.'

'I can't say it's not a relief. I was worried about leaving you in the lurch if I was passed fit.'

Dan leaned over and kissed her. That was the best part of their pre-dinner winding-down session. Feeling her lips against his and knowing that he could truly leave the working day behind him, not just stuff it in a convenient corner at the back of his mind until tomorrow.

'Why don't you leave the worrying to me?' He heard the oven beep. 'Dinner's ready…'

CHAPTER THIRTEEN

IT HAD BEEN a good week. Not without its challenges, both at the surgery and in the still, quiet hours of the night. But they were building something together, reinforcing and strengthening a structure that had seemed so precarious at first. It was easy and relaxed, supported by Dan's smile and his habit of taking each day as it came.

Then Friday happened. They were drinking their morning coffee, taking a breath before it was time to go to work, and a text pinged onto his phone.

'It's Mum.' He pressed his lips together in thought. 'She wants to know if I'd like to drive down to London and do some sightseeing with them tomorrow afternoon. Stay over for lunch on Sunday.'

'You should go. It'll be nice for you to see Charlie.' Alice knew that Dan had been missing him. If this weekend wasn't going to live up to her expectations and she'd spend it alone, that was okay.

'Will you come with me?'

Alice stared at him. 'You mean…? Dan, if we turn up together then aren't they going to ask questions? Won't Charlie be wondering what's going on?'

'He did see us kissing…'

'Just that one time, Dan. Hasn't he forgotten all about that?'

'Unlikely. He may not grasp the implications of things just yet, but there's nothing wrong with his memory. He might have told my parents, hence…' Dan picked up his phone, indicating the text. His mother had finished up by saying that, as always, he was welcome to bring a friend with him.

'What? I expect that Charlie's told your parents that he's seen you kissing someone, and so your mum's texted you and asked you to go down to London and bring a friend so that they can look me over?' Alice could feel herself blushing.

'That's the village talking, Alice. No one wants to look you over and pass judgement on you. Mum and Dad have always been pretty relaxed over that kind of thing, and when Nola died they became positively laissez-faire. We could say that we actually are just friends if you want; they knew Patrick. They won't ask, Mum will just make up the sofa bed for me and show you up to the spare room.'

'But…' Alice took a breath. 'Okay, so maybe

I *am* overreacting a bit. Bear with me on that one…'

Dan grinned. 'Of course.'

'How many more-than-friends have you taken with you to see them since you lost Nola?'

'None.'

'So I'm the first.' Alice couldn't help smiling at the thought.

'You know you are. Mum and Dad will be fine, they're not going to embarrass you. And Charlie… Well, he might, of course, but that's going to happen sooner or later. He knows that he can ask me about anything, that was the way we dealt with Nola's death.'

'Because if he's asking then he's ready to hear the answer?'

Dan nodded. 'Generally speaking. Sometimes I leave a few things out because I don't think he's ready to hear them yet, but I answer as honestly as I can.'

'And your mum and dad the same?'

'They were the ones who told me how to deal with the questions that Charlie was going to have when he was older. That I didn't need to sit him down and tell him everything, just talk about Nola and encourage him to ask. It's what they did themselves, with me.'

'Well…' Alice *was* curious about Dan's mother and father; he always spoke about them with such affection. And maybe this was a good opportunity to explain things to Charlie. 'I hope you know that I'll still be fretting about what to wear.'

'Come as you are?'

Alice plucked at the thin fabric of her sleeve. 'What, in your *Trees are for People* T-shirt?'

Dan grinned. 'No, that's just for me. Come as you will be when we arrive at the surgery.'

Twenty-four hours wasn't a long time to deal with her nerves, and the necessary ransacking of her wardrobe, but Dan had been maintaining his no-pressure approach. He'd tolerated an early start to the day on Saturday, and maintained his good humour through half an hour of taking things out of her overnight bag and then putting them back in again.

He was smiling as they got into his car, and Alice flipped to a music radio station as they drove. As they put some distance between themselves and the village, she felt a weight begin to lift from her shoulders. However much she tried to think of the village as home, however free and easy she felt in Dan's house, the burden was still there.

They left the motorway, heading for a suburb of north London. Streets grew narrower and shops were replaced by houses and greenery, and finally Dan slowed the car as he drove along an avenue lined with trees.

'This is where you grew up?' Alice took in the

houses, set back from the road behind well-tended front gardens. Unassuming, but this was clearly an affluent part of the sprawling city.

'Yes.'

'And you lived around here?'

'Not this road, we had a much smaller place, but it wasn't far. All the benefits of a capital city, just an hour away on the underground. But when you have to do that every day…'

'That's two hours you can't spend with Charlie.'

'Yep. It's a different life and it suited me once. I still love coming back—I want Charlie to feel at home here and I'd be more than happy if he decides to come to London to live. It's just not the place where I can give him what I think he needs right now.'

Alice nodded. Mallory Cross had grown in her imagination over the years, as if the bricks and mortar of the place had their own personality—and each one of them disapproved of her. Maybe that was a mistake—places were just places and they either reflected what a person wanted or they didn't.

Dan turned into a driveway, parking in front of one of the larger houses in the road. There was an agitated shimmer of net curtains and a few moments later the front door opened and Charlie came running out.

'Dad!'

Dan was already out of the car and he picked his son up, swinging him round and then hugging him tight. 'Hey there Charlie, I've been missing you. Has Grandad been behaving himself?'

Charlie nodded solemnly. 'So have I. We went to see the planets, Dad.'

'Yeah, I heard. And the fish… Which was bigger?'

Charlie considered the question. 'A fish is bigger than a planet. Although Grandad says that's because a planet is very far away.'

'I dare say he's right. Look who I brought with me…' Alice had stayed in the car to allow Charlie to greet his dad, but there was little choice in the matter now. Dan's parents were standing in the doorway and clearly they weren't expecting her to stay here until it was time to go tomorrow.

'Alice…' Dan had put Charlie back on his feet and he was running around to the passenger door. The boy stood back, watching as she got out of the car.

'Where's your stick?' Charlie peered behind her.

'I don't need it now.'

'Okay.' Charlie flung his arms around her waist, and Alice bent down to hug him.

'I bet you've been having a nice time…'

Charlie nodded, clearly unconcerned about telling her all about it, and took her hand. 'Come and see Grandma and Grandad.'

Dan was already on his way to the front door to hug his mother and father. Alice followed with Charlie, feeling Dan's fingers brush her arm in a gesture of reassurance.

'Alice, this is my mum and dad…'

'Ted and Norah,' Dan's father corrected him, stepping forward to shake her hand.

'Welcome, Alice, it's so nice to meet you.' Norah grasped Alice's hands between hers. 'I've got the kettle on, I expect you could murder a cup of tea after your drive. Or coffee, if you prefer?'

'Tea would be nice. Thank you.'

'Come and sit down…' Norah ushered her carefully into the hallway.

'It's okay, Mum. Alice's knee is a lot better now. Isn't it, Charlie?' Dan intervened.

Charlie nodded. 'When I *first* saw her, she couldn't walk.'

Norah laughed. 'Well, unless Alice has discovered a wonderful new cure for not being able to walk, I'm not sure that's quite right, Charlie. But Dan did tell us you were recovering from a broken patella, Alice, so Ted and I have been thinking about places to go that don't involve too much walking. I wonder if you'd like the London Eye?'

'I've never been, but I've always wanted to see it.'

'Wonderful.' Ted chuckled. 'Since we already have the tickets. Will you drive us there, Dan?'

'I'll be okay with the underground—isn't that

faster than driving?' Alice ventured. 'I've brought my stick with me. Only you'll have to make sure I don't get lost; I've only visited London a few times.'

'We won't let you wander away, will we, Charlie?' Dan grinned down at his son.

'No, Dad.' Charlie turned to Alice. 'We know the way; we'll take you there.'

Charlie obviously had a set of rules to follow for the underground. Keeping hold of his grandparents' hands and standing to the right on the escalators. He frowned at Alice when she stood too close to the yellow line on the platform and waited patiently to one side of the doors while everyone got off the train.

Meanwhile, Dan seemed to be breaking all of the rules. Inviting Alice to take his arm on and off the escalators and the trains was fair enough, but he seemed to feel no need to confine himself to that. She found herself strolling arm-in-arm with him, down the wide walkway towards the London Eye, which was entirely unnecessary. And when the glass capsule reached its highest point, his arm rested around her shoulders as he pointed out the landmarks beneath them.

But it was nice. If Ted and Norah noticed, they made no indication of having done so, and Charlie was too excited with this new experience to see anything but the wide blue sky above his head and the city beneath his feet. When Alice dared to take Dan's hand, he gave hers a squeeze and kept hold of it.

The family's evening meal turned out to be a laughing, easygoing affair, Ted sharing jokes with Alice, who was sitting next to him. Dan good-humouredly waved away his mother's comment about how like his father Charlie was becoming, but there was pride in his eyes.

As they sat drinking after-dinner coffee Charlie ran to a bookcase, pointing up at one of the shelves. 'Grandma, I want to show Alice…'

Norah shot to her feet. 'Not right now, Charlie. Shall we do that another time?'

'But…' Charlie frowned at his grandmother. 'Can't I do it now?'

'It's okay, Mum.' Dan turned to Alice. 'Charlie wants to show you my photograph album. The story of my life since I was four…'

That was why Norah had stopped Charlie so abruptly. Alice turned to her. 'I'd love to see it, Norah. If you don't mind.'

'Of course not.' Norah beamed at her, reaching the album down from the shelf and putting it into Charlie's outstretched arms. 'Careful with it, Charlie.'

Charlie put the album into her lap and climbed onto Dan's knee. Alice rested her hands on the cover. This was Dan's whole life…

'Where should I start?'

Dan smiled, settling Charlie down on his lap. 'The beginning's a good place.'

Alice opened the album, not sure what to expect. Would there be baby pictures? From what Dan had said she doubted it, and the first picture was one of a small boy in a school uniform that was very slightly big for him.

'Oh! This is you, Dan? You were so cute!'

Norah laughed suddenly, her smile broadening. 'He was, wasn't he, Ted? With that solemn look of his.'

Dan chuckled. 'I've grown out of both. Obviously.'

'Yes, clearly.' Alice shot him a smile, turning to the next picture. A summer's day in the garden, with a paddling pool. There was an older girl, whose dark hair and eyes were like her mother's and two boys who were engaged in a water fight. Dan was sitting in the pool, looking slightly less solemn but just as cute. Underneath, a picture of Dan, tipping water from a bucket over himself, a delighted smile on his face.

'I love this one. You took it?' she asked Norah.

'Yes, I'd been trying to get a good shot of him all afternoon, then suddenly he picked up the bucket and tipped the water out. I grabbed the camera and…it was pure chance that I even got him in the frame.'

'It looks perfect.' Alice looked up at Dan.

'Yeah. I remember that day too.' He smiled.

There were more pictures, of a little boy growing up and learning how to smile. Dan as an awkward adolescent and then as a young man, hugging his parents on his graduation day. Christmases and birthdays… Charlie obviously knew all of the pictures well, telling Alice the names of his aunts and uncles. Then Dan laid his hand on the page in front of her.

'Is that enough embarrassment for me now, Charlie?'

'No! I want to show my mum to Alice.'

Dan didn't move his hand. 'Another day, Charlie.'

'But she was very brave, Dad. She got a medal for…being brave. I want to show Alice.' Tears appeared in his eyes.

'You're getting tired, Charlie.' Norah tried to distract the boy. 'Would you like a story instead?'

'No!' Charlie buried his face in Dan's shirt, kicking against his leg. Dan winced, laying his hand on the boy's feet to still them.

'I'd like for Charlie to show me the pictures. If it's okay with you?' Alice murmured quietly.

The warmth in Dan's eyes told her that he'd stopped Charlie from turning the page to save her feelings, not his own. He nodded, smiling. 'Hey Charlie… Charlie. Are you listening? Alice says that she'd like to see your pictures of Mum.'

Charlie looked up at him, his tears forgotten

now. Then he leaned forward, turning the page of the album.

'That's my mum and dad.'

Dan looked so happy. So in love. Alice waited for the sting in the tail, those jealous feelings of seeing him with someone else, but they never came. All she felt was pleasure at seeing the solemn boy who'd grown into a man who knew how to smile.

'Your mum's very beautiful, Charlie.'

Charlie nodded. 'And she was very brave.' He didn't give Alice the chance to look at the other photos on the page, flipping it over to show a picture of Nola in her police officer's uniform.

'I can see that.' Nola was proud and brave. The kind of woman that Charlie and Dan deserved.

Charlie flipped the page again, hardly giving Alice a chance to study the photographs in front of her. 'That's when they got married…' He turned the page again. 'And that's me and my mum.'

Nola was glowing with happiness, a newborn child in her arms.

'That's you, Charlie?'

Charlie nodded solemnly. 'I've got more hair now.'

Dan chuckled. 'Yes, we can all see that. And you've got a lot more to say for yourself.' He hugged his son.

'Your mum loved you very much, Charlie. I can see it in her face.'

'Yes, she did. Didn't she, Dad?'

'Yes, Charlie. You were the apple of her eye.'

Charlie turned the page again. 'And that's me and Dad.'

The little boy looked as if he was attempting his first steps. And Dan's eyes were dead. As Charlie turned the pages, Alice saw Dan and Charlie in places that she knew in Mallory Cross, Charlie growing up and Dan beginning to live again. And the final photograph showed a group around a huge Christmas tree, in the room they were sitting in now. Dan was grinning broadly, trying to dissuade Charlie from touching the ornaments on the tree.

'That's my Auntie Kate and my cousins.' Charlie pointed to the dark-haired, petite woman with a toddler and a baby. 'Santa came here.'

'Santa always knows where you are, Charlie. He keeps a list.' Norah smiled at her grandson. 'Now, it's past your bedtime. Which story would you like?'

'Sonja and the Reindeer.'

'Okay.' Dan got to his feet, taking Charlie with him. 'That's a two-hander, Mum and I do the different voices. We may be a while.'

Charlie stopped for a kiss goodnight, from Alice and then Ted, and Dan swung him back up into his arms, following Norah. The room was suddenly silent, Ted looking at her thoughtfully. Alice wondered whether she'd done something wrong.

'That was a very gracious thing to do, Alice.' Ted finally spoke. Alice felt herself blush.

'I… It was nice of Charlie to show them to me.'

Ted nodded. 'Dan's always talked to Charlie about his mother. Even before the boy could understand. Charlie's very proud of her.' He got to his feet, flipping open a long, low credenza and taking out a cut-glass decanter. 'Will you join me? This is a very nice single malt.'

This was more than just hospitality; it was a gesture of friendship. Alice didn't usually drink whisky, but she'd make an exception. 'Thank you. I'd like to try it, perhaps just a splash…'

'So Dad offered you a glass of his best whisky?' Dan clearly felt that this was a singular privilege. 'What on earth are you wearing?'

'It's a nightie. What's wrong with it?' Alice looked down at the white Victorian-style nightdress that reached from her neck to her toes.

'It's not what you normally wear in bed.' He pulled his shirt over his head, reaching out to pluck at one of her full sleeves.

'How would you know? It might have been in my washing basket for the last week. And it's actually very warm in the winter. My friend bought it for me when I was in hospital, I was tired of those skimpy things they give you and wanted something a bit more—'

'Unbecoming?'

'A bit more modest. I didn't want to come here looking like a brazen temptress.'

'Well, you succeeded in that. Were you thinking of roaming the house in the small hours, in the hope that someone would catch sight of you and remark on your modesty? Although, on second thoughts, I do welcome the challenge.' Dan ran his fingers along the row of tiny buttons at her neck.

'They're just for show; they're sewn on the top of a strip of hook and loop tape. And don't give me a hard time—how would you have felt if we'd gone to see Dad and I'd asked him to let you share my bedroom?'

'Mortified. Undeserving. In fact, I'd have chickened out.' Dan wound his arms around her waist, kissing her. 'Don't listen to me. I'm grateful to you for having the sheer nerve to brave them *and* the photograph album. And my parents are showing every sign of adoring you.'

'Your mum and dad are both lovely—as you well know, Dan. And I'm glad I got to see the album. You've told me about all you've lost but… somehow, I never got the sense of it. I'm sorry.'

'Not your fault. I don't want anyone to get the sense of it, Alice. Not even me.'

'Charlie was saying that his mum was very brave…?'

'Yes, she was. Nola *did* get a medal, posthumously.'

'And Charlie doesn't know the details? Just that she was brave?'

'He's too young…' Dan sat down on the bed. 'She was called to a domestic dispute. But when she and her partner got there, things were a lot worse than they'd been led to believe—a man was holding his two children hostage in the house, threatening to kill them. She made a judgement call and went in—her partner said that the children seemed in immediate danger. Somehow, she got the children out, but…'

Alice sat down next to him. Waiting. Instinct told her that Dan needed to finish.

'Her partner said that she could have left with the children, but she stayed to try and talk the man down. He stabbed her…'

'Dan…' Her fingers reached out, but somehow couldn't find him. Then she felt his arm around her shoulders.

'It's okay.'

'Is it? Really?' His wife had died. Dan must have seen a faint echo of Nola's bravery in Alice's actions, when she'd jumped out of the helicopter to save a child. But he'd still supported her, helped her to work through it. Still fallen in love with her.

'I'm lucky to have found you, Alice.'

'That makes two of us. I consider myself lucky to have found you.' She put her arms around him, holding on tight. 'Do you suppose if we're *really* quiet…?' Tonight would be different. All about comfort and reminding each other why they were together, in the face of all the things that threatened to pull them apart.

'Are you telling me you'd take off that terrible nightie and come to bed with me?'

'I'd consider removing this very practical and warm nightie, yes.'

'I'm so happy to hear you say that…' They both jumped as the door handle rattled insistently.

'That's Charlie, isn't it?'

Dan nodded, going to the door and opening it. 'Hey Charlie. What are you doing out of bed?'

'I was frightened.'

'Yes?' Dan bent down, picking his son up. Charlie threw his arms around his dad's neck and Dan gently rubbed the boy's back. 'Is that something I can fix for you, or do you just want some company?'

'Company, Dad.'

Dan mouthed a *sorry* to Alice and she shook her head. 'This bed's big enough for three of us. You and Charlie take the duvet—I'll be fine with the comforter.' She picked up the warm woollen blanket that covered the bed. It would be more than enough for a summer's night.

It took a little careful positioning of arms and legs before Charlie was snuggled between them, with Dan's arm resting protectively across both Alice and Charlie.

'Not quite what we expected.' Dan grinned across at her.

'It's fine. It's just what I want.' If tonight was all about reassurance, then what better way was there? She blew Dan a kiss across the pillows.

'What I want, too…' He blew her a kiss back, smiling.

CHAPTER FOURTEEN

HIS MUM AND dad exchanged kisses with Alice when they left London after lunch on Sunday. They both hugged Charlie, and then they were on the road, back to Mallory Cross.

'Your mum's such a great cook. What am I going to do when they bring Charlie home, and I have to make lunch?' Alice leaned back in her seat.

'I said they had to stay for lunch. Didn't you notice the part where I neglected to mention who was going to cook it?'

She laughed. 'I was hoping you were leaving me a get-out. I cook up a good salad—that's easy enough, you just have to do lots of chopping and mixing.'

'So what's the difference? Cooking is just chopping and mixing, and then you put it into the oven. Or on the hob.'

'It's an extra layer of complication. Are you telling me that you'll cook?'

'We'll both cook. You can chop and mix, and I'll put it in the oven.'

'What did I do to deserve you, Dan Ryan?'

Dan laughed. 'Just keep thinking that. Then you might not start to wonder what I did to deserve you.'

When Dan unlocked his front door there was a copy of the local paper lying behind it. 'There's a note from Tabatha Green.'

'What does she say?' Alice rested her cheek against his arm. Now that they were home she seemed suddenly tired.

'*Marvellous response to your article. A dozen emails already. Looking forward to more, next month.*' Dan read the note aloud and Alice stifled a yawn.

'Is a dozen a lot?'

'When was the last time you emailed the local paper to say you liked an article? A dozen emails sounds good to me, and Tabatha's obviously pleased.' Alice didn't seem as happy as he'd expected. 'Are you all right?'

'Just tired. I didn't sleep much last night. Does Charlie come in to sleep with you a lot?'

'Not very much. If he's had a bad dream, usually, or something's upset him.'

Alice frowned. 'Was he upset because I was there with you?'

'More likely he was happy to see you and

wanted a sleepover. I should have taken him back to his own room.'

'I'm glad you didn't. I didn't sleep because I was too busy watching you both and deciding which one of you is the cutest.'

Dan chuckled. 'Charlie, definitely. Why don't you go upstairs and lie down for a couple of hours?'

She curled her arm around his neck. 'I might just do that. I didn't get much sleep on Friday night either, worrying about what your parents might think of me…'

'They loved you. You worry too much about what other people think.'

'Maybe…' Alice rested her head on his chest, and Dan couldn't resist waltzing her gently to the bottom of the stairs. 'What if I get bad dreams, Dan?'

'I'd better come with you, and make sure you don't.'

When she lay down on the bed and Dan curled his arms around her, Alice fell asleep almost straight away. The regular sound of her breathing, the warmth of her body next to him, made Dan doze, but he couldn't sleep. Time was a precious commodity, and it was slipping through his fingers all too fast.

In another ten days' time Alice would be making another trip down to London, alone this time. She'd insisted it *would* be alone, and Dan suspected that whatever the results of her fitness-for-work assessment, Alice would be wanting some time alone to process them, and he'd reluctantly agreed.

Dan needed some time to process, too. He'd gone into this knowing that it wouldn't be easy. That his need for a stable home for him and Charlie, where he could protect himself and his son from loss, weren't a good fit with the loss of trust and respect that Alice had experienced here in the village. And the compelling honesty that had grown between them had brought new challenges. Alice's bravery was a lot like Nola's, and Dan couldn't help fearing for her.

But if their lives didn't fit together, then their love did. Perfect and seamless, as if they'd been made for each other. At times like this, that was all that mattered.

Alice sat in the pleasant office. She'd been up early, and Dan had driven her to the station, to catch the train to London that would connect with her train down to the air ambulance headquarters in Sussex.

He'd been silent in the car, which was a relief because Alice hadn't felt much like talking either. Whatever happened today would change things for both of them. But as her train drew into the platform, Dan's kiss had been just the same.

And now, after a barrage of tests and fitness assessments and a comprehensive readiness for work interview, she was facing the final hurdle. Zoe Ballantyne would be giving her the verdict.

'Things seem to have been going very well for you since we last saw you. You've made really good progress physically, and you've clearly been taking steps to ground yourself and stay in touch with a medical environment without compromising your recovery.'

Alice hadn't mentioned the part about wading around in rivers. Zoe didn't need to know that and there had been no choice. 'Things could go better…' She smiled at Zoe.

Zoe smiled back. 'I'm glad to hear you say that. I was wondering whether your enthusiasm for the air ambulance service might have waned a little.'

Never. Being back here had made that very clear to Alice. All that she and Dan had done together had been about recovery—hers and his together. There was no going back on that.

'I want to go back to work.'

Zoe nodded. 'Then I'm very happy to say that you've been passed as fit for work.'

Alice felt tears rise in her eyes. Zoe reached for a paper handkerchief and handed it to her. 'Thank you, Zoe…'

'It's my pleasure. We need people like you, Alice.' Zoe tactfully left her a moment to wipe the tears from her eyes. 'Now. I have a few forms for you to sign, and perhaps we can sort out some timings…'

Now the next challenge. Alice knew that Dan was eager for news, and she'd escaped out into the open air and found a bench where she could sit undisturbed with her takeaway coffee. Taken a breath, and texted him. Dan had replied immediately, with smiles and congratulations.

Her train was delayed and it was seven o'clock before Alice arrived back at the station closest to Mallory Cross. But Dan was waiting on the platform, along with Charlie, who was brandishing what looked like a balloon helicopter.

'Charlie!' She stretched her arms out with an exuberance she didn't feel, and gave the boy a hug. 'Did your dad make that for you?'

'Dr McIntyre did the balloons and I drew on them.' Charlie held out the string affixed to the model. 'It's for you.'

'That's beautiful, thank you.' Alice examined the helicopter. Along the sides, someone had drawn a neat row of windows, and Charlie's more erratic hand had added faces. 'Is that you at the front? In the pilot's seat?'

Charlie nodded. 'And that's you.' He pointed to an extra-large face at the side, attached to an arm which was brandishing something.

'You're holding your stethoscope.' Dan came to the rescue.

'Ah. Well, yes, I would be.' Alice straightened, kissing him. Dan's kiss was the same as it had been this morning, the same as it had always been. If Zoe had witnessed it, then no doubt she would have concluded that he was responsible for the 'grounding' that had taken place over the last few weeks.

'That's *enough*, Dad…' Charlie tugged at his hand. He'd responded well to the idea that Alice had practically moved in with them, no doubt primed by his grandparents. But Dan and Alice were always careful to reassure him that he hadn't been pushed to one side.

'It's never enough,' Dan murmured to her, before letting her go. 'What do you say we go out for dinner, eh? Celebrate.'

Did he really want to celebrate their parting? Or was Dan just making a good job of accepting something he knew that Alice wanted?

'Can we go tomorrow? They really put me through my paces and I don't think I could do a celebration justice this evening.'

'Of course.' Dan turned to Charlie. 'It's burgers tomorrow, then.'

Burgers were the new once-a-week rule. Charlie had decided that he didn't like pizza after all, and Dan had been testing out a few recipes at home, as well as checking out some restaurants that included burgers in their menu.

'Yes! Burgers, Dad. Alice likes burgers.'

'Almost as much as you? Let's go home and find a place to put Alice's helicopter where we can all see it, eh?'

Charlie had been settled down to sleep, and it was their time now. Dan could ask Alice what was going on—she'd been very tight-lipped about the arrangements for her return to work when he'd asked over dinner.

When he made his way quietly downstairs, Alice was examining the helicopter. 'This is really good. I didn't know that John made balloon figures.'

'Me neither. Did you know he speaks Japanese?'

'No. Is there no end to the things he can do?'

Dan shook his head. 'If there is, then I haven't found it. Apparently, he and Adele spent a year in Japan when he was newly qualified. He claims his Japanese is very rusty, but he managed to communicate with a couple of Japanese tourists who walked into the surgery last week.'

'Oh. What was the matter with them?'

'Nothing, they were lost, and wanted to know the way to Cambridge… Are you playing for time, Alice?' He sat down on the sofa next to her.

She shot him an innocent look and he raised an eyebrow in reply.

'I've been wondering how to talk with you about this, Dan.'

'Words… Sentences, even.' Dan put his arm around her shoulders. 'It can't be that bad, can it?'

From the look on her face, Alice obviously thought that it was. Dan ignored the fears that were tugging at his sleeve. Alice always fretted about what people would think, and Dan had tried to dissuade her from second-guessing him more than once.

'I don't know—it's good and it's bad…'

Dan waited. Silence was his best option now. Alice would come out with it in her own time.

'They've given me a tentative start date… The doctor says that if my knee continues to improve the way it has, the medical for active service in another month will be a formality. They want me to come back a little early, though, as there's a round of interviews for new candidates which will be starting in ten days' time. I'll be helping select who goes forward to the next stage, and then talking to them informally about the realities of working on an air ambulance team…'

Suddenly a tear rolled down her cheek. 'I'm so happy with all of that, Dan…'

'Good. So am I.'

'But I'm not happy about what that means for us. The time we've spent together means more than I can say—you must know that…' Alice gulped down her tears, clinging to him. 'I don't want you to feel that I'm leaving you.'

So that was it. Dan was thankful that Alice couldn't see the smile that was tugging at his lips, although perhaps she heard the way his heart had leapt into a new and stronger beat.

'We talked about this. You're not leaving, you're going back. I'm staying here. We each made a decision, didn't we?'

'Yes, but…' It seemed that Alice could look at him again, and her golden gaze searched his face. If she was looking for insincerity then she wouldn't find it. 'I'm the one who's actually packing my bags. It feels like leaving.'

It was time for some straight talking. 'Look, Alice. We both have our own lives, and that means a great deal, for a lot of reasons. I respect yours, just as you respect mine. If we didn't then we'd truly be leaving each other, wouldn't we?'

She nodded. 'I was hoping you'd see it that way.'

'Give me some credit, then. I'm going to miss you like crazy and I'll even worry about you a little.' Perhaps slightly more than a little, but Alice really didn't need to know that. 'But I want you to go.'

She flung her arms around his neck. 'And I want you to stay here, Dan—it's the right place for you and Charlie. Even if it *does* mean that

I'll be missing you too. Every last little bit of you…' Her smile told him exactly which bits of him Alice had in mind.

'Yeah? We have another ten days…'

Alice smiled, kissing him. 'And ten nights.'

'There's a lot we can do in that time.' Dan was already feeling it. 'And after that…there's a lot to be said for anticipation.'

She caressed his cheek. 'And you, sir, are the master of anticipation…' Alice stilled suddenly. 'We're in this together, Dan.'

'Of course we are.'

Dan hoped so. And if he and Alice really could achieve the impossible, then now was the time to prove it…

CHAPTER FIFTEEN

THE LAST TEN days had been so perfect, spiced with the knowledge that she'd be going back to the job that she loved, and that Dan supported the idea. That they might be putting some distance between each other but neither of them would be leaving. They had a future.

He'd arranged a surprise party for her, on the Friday evening before she was due to go, at the new restaurant that they'd visited on her first weekend back in Mallory Cross.

'Did you ever think that you'd leave the village like this?' Dan murmured as he leaned towards her.

'No. Never.' How different everything was from the last time they'd been here—there were two large tables full of friends, all talking and laughing together. 'I thought that I might spend a few days, settling the things I needed to sort out, and then sneak away again. Am I doing the right thing, Dan?'

'Hey. Hold your nerve. We agreed that we'd

work things out and…we just have to give it a chance. Do you want this job?'

'Yes, I really do.'

'Well, that's all we need to know right now.'

The following morning, Dan loaded up the car with everything she wanted to take with her to Sussex and they drove down together, leaving Charlie with Molly and her husband, who could always be counted on to have somewhere interesting to visit at the weekend.

Her small house smelled musty, after having been closed up for so long. 'Shame I didn't have Rosie Franklin to come and look after the place while I was gone.' Alice was already beginning to miss the quiet gleam of her father's house. The bright, airy welcome of Dan's.

'I love your home.' He was looking around the small hallway and through the open door into the sitting room.

'You do?' That was a surprise. Dan's house was so orderly and coordinated.

'Yeah. What do you call that colour?'

'Um…' Alice regarded the sitting room wall thoughtfully. 'Pinky mushroom?'

Dan nodded. 'Did the cast-iron fireplace come with the property?'

'No, Dad bought it back in the nineties, when everyone was throwing them out. He couldn't find a place for it at home, and when I bought the house he gave it to me. I had to scrape about twenty coats of paint off it, but when I'd done that and polished it up it looked really nice.'

'This place does remind me of Patrick. Only a rather more concentrated version of his eclectic taste.'

'It's what I grew up with. I guess I must have taken it with me when I left.' Alice had always regarded her house as slightly idiosyncratic, but eclectic was a much kinder word.

'I wouldn't know how to put these colours together.' Dan wandered through into the kitchen. 'You may have noticed that I chickened out of colours and had the whole house painted off-white.'

'It's nice. Light, airy… Everything matches and fits into the space properly.'

'That's because everything was bought for the house. I've been travelling light over the last few years. Charlie's the one who's the collector, and he already orders things differently from me. He puts them in order of what they look like, rather than what they do.' He turned around suddenly to face her. 'The more I know about you, the more I think that we're very different.'

'Isn't that a good thing?' Alice asked.

He wrapped his arm around her waist, pulling her close. 'Not sure I've come to a conclusion yet. But I always find that I want to know more.'

* * *

Dan had to leave in time to get back and spend the evening with Charlie, which meant that Alice couldn't introduce him to her moss-coloured bedroom, one wall of which was covered with flower prints that she'd picked up in various places, over the years. His appreciation of her house had made Alice see it in a different light. A warmer, happier kind of light that danced around her even though Dan was gone.

She could get down to the realities of missing him, now. Next weekend was taken up by interviews for candidates who couldn't get time off work during the week, and Dan would have to be at the surgery with John, to handle the weekend cover for the four practices in the area. But Dan would be making the journey down to see her in two weeks' time.

They'd agreed that time spent together would be theirs alone. No phone calls or texts in the intervals between Dan's patients and her interviewees, because it might take a whole day of missed calls and texts to find five minutes when they were both free. When Alice sat down in front of her laptop, knowing that Charlie would be in bed and there was nothing to interrupt them, she felt a frisson of excitement.

'You dressed up.' His grin appeared on the screen.

'So did you.' Dan looked *very* handsome, in a

dark blue shirt that always made his eyes seem more mesmerising. 'That's okay, it is Saturday night.'

Alice wondered whether he might be induced to undo a couple more buttons on his shirt, and decided not to ask. Undoing them herself was much more fun, and he'd be here soon enough. He might be her lover but he was her best friend as well.

He'd obviously come to the same conclusion and didn't refer to her buttons either, although the look in his eyes told Alice that it had crossed his mind.

'So, what's been happening? Are you settling in?' Dan asked.

'Yes, Toby and the team came round yesterday evening and Toby brought my car back—he's been keeping it in his garage while I've been away, and giving it a run-around every now and then. I nearly didn't recognise it; he polished it up and it's running better than it ever did. Toby's our pilot and pretty good with engines.'

'So you'll be driving soon?'

Alice nodded. 'They all piled in and we took it down to the airfield for me to give it a go. Adam, who's our paramedic, insisted on a few emergency stops, and they were fine. I'll have to be signed off by my doctor, but I have an appointment on Monday evening and since she already has the results of my medical, that'll be a formality. It'll be a lot easier getting into work when I can drive.'

'And the interviews?'

'I'm learning a lot. At first, everyone seemed so perfect and well qualified, but the other people on the board have taught me what to look for. And guess what…?' Alice had been saving the best until last. 'I went up with my crew on Wednesday!'

Dan stared at her. 'In the helicopter? I thought you weren't signed off as fit for active service yet.'

'I'm not, but I am signed off to work and that includes working as a doctor. It was a transfer between hospitals and so there was no on-site treatment to be done—our patient was accompanied by medical staff onto and off the helicopter. Adam was there as well and he's very capable of handling everything I can, and I was just aboard to help out if there was an emergency. Which there wasn't.'

Dan was clearly trying not to frown. Something was bugging him. 'But what about the doctor who's filling in for you?'

'David was in A&E. He broke a couple of fingers.'

'What?' Dan had given up on the frown and it had turned into a look of alarm. 'He was injured on duty?'

Now she got it. One doctor injured on duty was an accident. Two might be classed as carelessness.

'The door of the cafeteria slammed on his fingers, Dan.'

He smiled suddenly. 'Sorry. Easy mistake to make.'

Was he referring to a badly adjusted door closer, or did Dan mean his own mistake? Perhaps it was better to let that slide.

'So, what's been happening back in Mallory Cross? Do you have any gossip for me?'

Dan chuckled. 'I thought you didn't like gossip…'

They'd spent two hours online, talking until they were both yawning. And Dan's goodbyes were as affectionate as she could have wished. But there were still a few lingering doubts…

Maybe Alice should have been a little more careful. It was easy for her to view her job as no more risky than any other. Everyone was trained to put safety first; there was a rigorous maintenance routine for all of the helicopters. Alice had dealt with a few difficult patients, but she doubted it was as many as the average A&E nurse encountered in their working week. Probably fewer than Dan came across in the course of his work. And, by any measure of likelihood, car travel was a great deal more risky than helicopter travel, particularly when there were two pilots, both of whom were very highly trained.

But none of those lines of reasoning meant anything to Dan. He'd lost the parents who should have loved him, and then a wife who *had* loved him. If worrying about Alice was a measure of how deeply he felt for her, then that was cold comfort.

She should be more careful. It was good to see him, to speak with him, when they couldn't be together, but it had its downsides. This was the first lesson she needed to learn, in their journey towards being together.

Dan wasn't sleeping. And when he did sleep, he dreamt and woke up in a cold sweat. He'd always felt that he'd lost Nola, but now the word *lost* sounded too careless, and far too arbitrary. The truth of it was that she'd been one of the people who ran towards a crisis instead of away from it. And Alice was one of those people, too. It was one of the many things he loved about her.

He'd supported her in going back to work, and if he had that to do over again, he would have done more to help her recover, not less. Dan didn't regret a thing. Not falling in love with Alice. And not encouraging her to leave. Everything he'd said to her was true, and he believed wholeheartedly that if they stopped respecting each other's fears about the past, and hopes for the future, then they would truly be abandoning each other.

'Dad…' Charlie was sitting on a high stool in the kitchen, rolling out pastry. 'Time to stop.'

'I'll finish off.' Dan picked up the stool, with Charlie on it, and moved it a couple of feet along the countertop. 'We won't use the bit with the holes in it, but the rest is really good.'

'I didn't make the holes. The pastry did.'

'Yeah. Pastry'll do that.'

Charlie nodded sagely. 'You can come and sleep in my room, Dad.'

Because the pastry had holes in it? Dan shook his head, trying to clear the fatigue that three nights of broken sleep had left behind them. Clearly, he wasn't keeping up with Charlie's tendency to discard one subject when he was done with it and pick up another.

'You want me to?'

'No.'

Okay. Charlie clearly had something on his mind. He'd heard nothing from Eve or the school to account for it and Charlie was usually happy to sleep alone in his room.

'Is something bothering you? Are you missing Alice?'

'No, Dad. Alice has important helicopter things. She won't forget me.' Charlie could be remarkably pragmatic at times. 'If you miss her, you can come and sleep in my room.'

His beautiful son… 'Thank you, Charlie, that's a really nice thought. But I'm okay. Alice has helicopter things and we have things to do here.'

Charlie nodded. 'I got a gold star today…'

Charlie's chatter about his day at school only seemed to require his agreement, and Dan's thoughts floated back to *helicopter things.* Alice would always have helicopter things. Maybe that meant he'd have to wave a fond goodbye to the thought of a good night's sleep.

Alice had promised him that she'd be there, to see this through. But maybe the thing that they'd both failed to see, in the heat of their embraces, was that the best way was out and not through…

Dan was coming this weekend and she couldn't wait. But even though she left work on time, she saw his car parked outside her house when she got home. She tapped on the window and Dan got out of the driver's seat.

'You're early…' Perhaps he hadn't been able to wait to see her either.

'Yes, I took the afternoon off work. How's your week been?'

'Good. Busy. The interviews are finished now, and we have to draw up a shortlist. There's been a lot of interest, and we want to give everyone fair consideration.' Alice popped her head inside the car and then realised that Dan had come alone. 'Where's Charlie? Is he okay?'

'Charlie's fine. I needed to see you, but I have to get back this evening.'

'Okay.' Perhaps Alice should ask whether she ought to pack, because surely she'd be going back to Mallory Cross with Dan, but instinct stopped her. 'Well, come in and I'll make some tea.'

He followed her to the front door, and then to the kitchen, without a word. Alice felt the euphoria of her first fortnight back at work begin to dissolve as panic started to crawl up her spine. She put the kettle on, and then turned around to face him.

'What's up, Dan? Has something happened?'

He shook his head, leaning back against the countertop. Keeping as far away from her as the size of the small kitchen allowed. 'Alice, I think we should take a break…'

'A break! Dan?' His words hit her like a sharp blow to the chest. 'What sort of break?'

'A long one. Probably permanent.'

She could fling herself at him. Tell him this was crazy, and that everything was okay. Something about the coolness in his eyes stopped her.

'What's all this about, Dan?'

'We promised that we'd both be there for each other, and find a way through. I meant that, and I know you did too.' Dan brushed his fingers across his face. 'But maybe we have to face the fact that we're putting a lot of effort into something that can't work. I thought it could…'

'And what? You've driven all the way down here just to say that, and then drive back again?'

'Would you prefer I'd phoned? Or texted, maybe.' His face darkened, and she saw his jaw set hard.

A phone call or a text would have been the coward's way out and Dan was no coward. Anyone worth their salt would face a girl if he was going to break up with her. *Break up.* Just thinking the words made her feel sick.

'I'd really prefer it if you gave me some clue about what's going on, Dan. It's been two weeks since I saw you last, not a millennium. What's changed?'

'If it were just a matter of finding somewhere we could both be happy, then…' Dan shrugged. 'But it's not about that. You've made a life for yourself, here, doing important work. It's where you need to be. But I lie awake at night worrying about whether something will go wrong and you'll be hurt. I reckoned I could cope with that, but… I'm sorry, Alice, I just can't. It consumes me.'

'And you want to give up, without even trying?'

'Do you want to keep trying until we hurt each other so badly that there's no way back from it?'

She stared at him. They'd made promises, agreed that somehow they'd navigate their way back to each other. And Dan couldn't fail. He couldn't go back to being the boy with the sad eyes, the man with the empty expression of pain.

'So you've been lying to me.' Hurt sharpened her tongue.

'I said we'd find a way. I think that we just have.'

'No, Dan. *You* just have, not me. You told me to come back here, and now you're saying you can't commit to that.'

Anger showed in his face. 'You've never made any secret about wanting to get as far away from Mallory Cross as quickly as you can, and you've always wanted to be back with the air ambulance service. I said that we should respect what the past has made of us both, and I still believe that.'

'I understand that, Dan, I really do. But I just wish we could have…' What? Done something different? Neither of them could *be* anything different. Alice was suddenly breathless, as if she'd been plunged into cold water. Trying to reach for the sunshine but sinking fast.

His anger seemed to drain out of him, and she saw tenderness in his face. That hurt more than anything they could say to each other. 'Don't you see, now? Why we can't be together?'

She felt tears flood her eyes. 'Dan, you're hurting me. I want you to go.'

He was still for a moment and then he turned, walking towards the door. Alice tried to think of something, anything that might bring him back.

If she could contrive to be struck by lightning some time in the next thirty seconds that might do it—he'd have to rush back and save her.

Too late. Dan was already closing the front door behind him. Alice picked up one of the plates from the drainer, wondering whether the sound of broken crockery might be appropriate for the moment. The moment when she could feel her heart being torn apart in her chest.

The plate slipped from her fingers and hit the floor. Alice walked out of the kitchen, broken shards crunching beneath her feet. Everything that Dan had said was right. Everything she'd said was right, too. That was why there was nothing to do now but go upstairs, lie on her bed and cry.

Dan was driving on unfamiliar roads, nursing a heart that had nowhere to go. He had to stop and take a breath.

He'd known that this would be hard, but he'd had to come. Even though he knew that Alice would fight him, that she'd throw every hard truth that she could in his direction. That was Alice and he loved her for the way she never gave up, even if he'd wished that she might accept the inevitable with a little more peace of mind and a little less rage.

He pulled up outside a coffee shop, going inside to order a large coffee. He probably should eat, and the only thing that didn't make him feel slightly sick was a muffin. Walking past the seats, he got back into his car.

Ten minutes later, he was back on the road. The M25 would be busy at this time on a Friday evening, and he took a route through London instead of the orbital motorway, twisting and turning through backstreets. Then he headed for home, picking Charlie up from Eve Morrison's house. The boy was drowsy, half asleep in his arms as he carried him out to the car.

Carefully, deliberately, he carried Charlie up to his bedroom, easing him into his pyjamas then putting him to bed. He could go back downstairs, but there was nothing there to interest him. Dan went to his own room, changing into a pair of sweatpants and a T-shirt. Maybe he'd burn the clothes he'd been wearing; they were witness to far too much…

Instinct led him back to Charlie's room. He gathered the sleeping boy up, careful not to wake him.

'Hey there, Charlie,' he whispered, 'I'm a little afraid, and I don't think that you can fix it. I'd like some company, though.'

The boy didn't respond. Dan carried him through to his own room, lying down with him, and Charlie snuggled into the warmth of his body.

'Dad…?'

'Yeah. Go back to sleep, Charlie. Everything's fine and the morning's waiting for you.'

His pillow was wet with tears. This wouldn't last. Some day the ache would subside and he'd start to live again. Not yet, though. Maybe not for a long while.

CHAPTER SIXTEEN

'HEY, STRANGER. Can I help you?' Toby was sitting in a deckchair outside the cafeteria, drinking a cup of tea. At any minute now the phone was going to ring, because he was holding a foil-wrapped sandwich.

'Just passing through.' Alice summoned up a smile. She kept walking, and heard Toby's voice behind her.

'Hey! Help a guy out!'

So Toby wasn't going to let up on her. Alice knew she'd been like a zombie for the last two days and even though she wasn't working with them yet, the team must have noticed. She turned, walking back to the empty deckchair beside him.

'I've only got an hour for lunch. What do you want, Toby?'

'You've got anywhere else to go?'

Not really. Alice couldn't think of one place she needed to be. Not for the next ten years, at least. She sat down, looking up at the clear blue sky. Good weather for flying, but she didn't much want to be in the air either.

'What's up?' Toby took a sip of his tea. 'Nothing, Toby.' His voice went up an octave, mimicking hers. 'I know there's something the matter, Alice. A trouble shared…'

'*Really*, Toby?' Alice saved him the trouble of anticipating her next line.

'Yeah. Really, Alice. Come on, spill. I haven't got all day, the hotline's going to ring any minute now. What is it that I really don't need to know about?'

Alice didn't answer.

'Let me see, now. You drag yourself off to some village at the back end of nowhere—'

Alice opened her mouth to protest that Mallory Cross was *not* the back end of nowhere, and Toby waved her into silence.

'Now's not the time to start talking, Alice. You take yourself off to the village for two weeks, saying you're not going to spend a moment more there than you have to, and end up staying for over a month. You come back happy and as fit as a flea. Then you're off duty for the weekend and suddenly you're…'

'As miserable as a squashed flea?' Alice twisted her mouth into a wry smile. As usual, Toby had summed up the situation.

'Who is he, Mr Tall-Dark-and-Handsome?'

'He's blond. Blue eyes.'

'Ah.' Toby nodded. 'You've got it bad, then.'

'What, because I happened to notice he had blue eyes?' The colour of the afternoon sky. Ever changing and ever beautiful.

'*Had* blue eyes. What's he done, changed his eye colour?'

'No. He's gone, and he's not coming back. The village is his territory now and the rest of the world's mine—we won't be bumping into each other any time soon.'

Toby puffed out a breath. 'You're going to make me do *all* of the work, aren't you. Tall, *blue*-eyed and handsome, buries himself in some nameless village—'

'Mallory Cross, Toby. You know where I come from.'

'Don't interrupt. He's got kids?'

As usual, Toby had worked it out. Maybe watching the sky, knowing what it might do next, would help a person out with the mysteries of human behaviour.

'Just the one. His name's Charlie and he's only five. He gave me his balloon helicopter when I passed my medical.'

'My kind of kid. No one ever gave *me* a balloon helicopter.'

'Don't make it sound as if you're all alone under a vast sky…' Outside of work, Toby's wife and three young daughters were his world.

‘I send them postcards.’

‘Postcards? I never knew that. What kind of postcards?’

Toby got up abruptly, leaving his sandwich behind and walking into the building. Alice followed him to the locker room, intrigued. He opened his locker, taking out an envelope from between two carefully folded T-shirts, and handed her its contents—a fat pile of postcards.

Alice flipped through them. There were the obligatory scenes of helicopters, probably bought from the air ambulance fundraising website. Various scenes from around Sussex and…

‘Paris? Greece?’

‘I buy them when we’re on holiday. Save them up.’

‘And send them to Marie and the girls? But you’re home every evening.’ It was nice, though. A postcard dropping through the letterbox, just to let them know that they were always in Toby’s thoughts.

‘There’s something about a postcard. Marie likes them and so do the kids.’

‘I’m sure they do. Toby, you old romantic.’ She nudged him in the ribs and he frowned.

‘Tell anyone and you’re a dead woman.’

‘My lips are sealed.’

‘And another thing. In my long and varied experience of break-ups—’

'Don't start on that, Toby. We all know it took you a while to find your one and only.'

'Marie was worth waiting for. And in my long and varied experience, even if you generally don't stay friends, it's nice to think that you might. A postcard will do that for you and it's easier to put under your pillow than social media.' Toby raised a querying eyebrow.

Alice shook her head. She really didn't want to be friends with Dan; that would be too excruciating. 'I don't think we're ever going to get to that point. I'm going to have to stick to my side of the world, and Dan…' She hadn't meant to say his name. Alice felt tears rise in her eyes and blinked them back, but she wasn't fast enough.

Toby shook his head, as if he'd just found irrefutable proof that things were bad. He could have saved himself the trouble. Things were *really* bad.

'Think about it, Alice. If you can't bear to even say his name, you might just wonder what it is that you're both running from…'

'Thanks, Toby. That's terrible advice. Can I have one of your postcards, please?'

'Yeah. Not the ones with the dogs, my youngest likes those…'

It had been a week. Dan had ticked each day off the calendar as if it had been a prison sentence, but there was no point in even thinking about the possibility of an early release just yet.

He'd known just what to do. He'd sat down with Charlie, explaining that Alice was a heroine. A lot of people needed saving and she had to go and do it, even if she'd miss her best friend.

'Who's Alice's best friend, Dad?'

'You are, Charlie. Alice won't forget you, but we have to let her go, even if we miss her.'

Charlie nodded. 'Okay. When she's finished saving people, will she come back to see us?'

No. Almost certainly not. 'Maybe one day, Charlie.' In Charlie's world, *one day* would be lost amongst the family and friends that Dan had surrounded his son with. In his world, *one day* was a bitter remembrance of something that would never come.

And then, two days later, the envelope dropped through the door. It was addressed to Dan and he opened it, still shaking off yet another sleepless night. Then his heart suddenly pumped out a wake-up call.

There was a postcard inside, addressed to Charlie. An air ambulance helicopter, silhouetted against the sky. And the message on the back, in Alice's neat handwriting, was for her friend Charlie.

A tear dropped from his eye onto the postcard and Dan brushed it away quickly, before it made a mark. Alice had gone. Maybe she was still angry with him and maybe not, but she wasn't angry with Charlie. And she was showing it in the only way she could—addressing the letter to Dan so that he could choose whether to give it to his son.

There really wasn't any choice. Even though this hurt, Dan murmured a *thank-you* to Alice and walked to the bottom of the stairs.

'Hey, Charlie. What are you doing up there? Breakfast's ready and you've got a postcard…'

In a month there had been four postcards, arriving usually on a Saturday. No mention of what Alice was doing, but they were enough. Dan could stand his own pain if Charlie knew that Alice hadn't forgotten him.

Charlie had wanted to write back, and Dan had got him a pack of plain postcards that he could draw a picture of his own on, and written the words 'To Alice, love Charlie' on the other side for the boy to trace over with his crayons. As he lifted Charlie up to drop it into the postbox, he sent his own love along with his son's.

And then, after a month, there was more. Dan opened the now-expected envelope and when he withdrew the postcard a leaflet fluttered out, for an air ambulance open day, two weeks from now. On the back, Alice had written a message.

To Charlie and friend(s). If you can come, I'll book a ride for you on my helicopter. Love, Alice.

And friend(s)? What did that mean? Dan's first reaction at being demoted to the '*and friends*' category began to soften—all she was doing was trying to give him a choice. If he wanted to bring Charlie himself, he could, but he could enlist someone else to go. Dan folded the leaflet carefully and put it into his pocket.

'Charlie… Postcard!'

Ella Harper probably wasn't the first person Dan wanted to see on a Monday morning. He'd put aside enough time to go through the results of Ella's blood tests carefully. Her cholesterol was high, and when he'd taken her blood pressure that was also elevated. Something had to be done and Dan wasn't expecting it to be easy to convince her.

'Ella. Are you listening to me?' Ella had seemed unconcerned when he'd outlined the changes in diet and lifestyle she needed to make. 'We can reduce both your cholesterol level and your blood pressure with medication, but it would be good if you could see what you can do yourself first. In any case, you'd improve your general health.'

Ella pressed her lips together, folding the fact sheets he'd given her into her handbag and snapping it shut. 'I suppose all of this means I'll have to find some new recipes.'

Ella had always been Patrick's patient, and he'd

joked that should she ever present herself at the surgery when he wasn't there, his best advice to Dan was to show no fear. Rumour had it that Ella had been a bit of a firebrand in her youth, and Patrick had found that she appreciated a straightforward approach.

'There's always the library.' Dan handed her the list of useful internet resources that he'd drawn up. 'Didn't I see the librarian showing you how to use the computer there the other day? If you can do that, then you can do this.'

Was that a smile? 'So I have to do this all on my own, do I?'

'No, I'm here to help you in any way I can. But I can't make these changes for you.' Dan smiled back at Ella.

'You think I don't know about change?' Ella seemed to be taking pleasure in this now, and on balance enjoying a visit to the doctor was something to be encouraged. 'I remember when a man first set foot on the moon, I was watching it on next door's television with my mother. I don't recall seeing you on the coach we took down to London to march for equal pay for women either.'

'You were a part of that? That's something to be proud of.'

'I was a part of a great deal more than that...' Ella raised an eyebrow.

'I'd like to hear about it, when we have more time. But getting back to your cholesterol level...'

Ella waved her hand at him dismissively. 'Let's see what we can do about that, shall we? So I can live to be a hundred.'

Dan wouldn't put it past Ella to outlive everyone in the village, himself included, just from sheer bloody-mindedness. 'I'm a lot more interested in you living *well* until you're a hundred.'

Ella fixed him with a knowing look. 'In my experience, living well always does seem to involve change. You might like to remember that.'

'Thanks for the advice.' Dan wasn't entirely sure who was advising who now, but Ella's words had struck a chord. Maybe he should listen to her a little better in future.

'You're welcome. I'll see you in a month's time?'

'I'll look forward to it.' Dan had been so wrapped up in the way things were that he'd forgotten about how they might change. And suddenly, he didn't want to be left behind.

He heard the door to John's consulting room open and close and got to his feet, grabbing the leaflet that Alice had sent from his desk drawer.

'John, got a minute?' He handed him the leaflet and John read it through, holding his hand up to silence Dan when he tried to interrupt. John always read everything through from start to finish and Dan supposed that was why he was always such a mine of information about anything you'd care to name.

'Are you going?'

That was the question that Dan had been pondering for the last two days, and now he had the answer. 'Yes. I don't suppose you'd like to come along? Does Annabel like helicopters?' John's eldest grandchild was the same age as Charlie and the two of them played together regularly.

'No idea. She likes to go places, and I dare say she will when we get there.'

'So you'll come? With Annabel?'

John put the leaflet down on his desk, looking at him with mild puzzlement. 'Yes, we'd love to, thank you. Are you going to give Alice a call?'

'No.' That was probably a step too far. Dan's heart had almost burst out of his chest just at the thought of hearing her voice on the phone.

'You want me to call her?' John picked up his phone, searching through his extensive list of contacts.

'Don't we just turn up?'

'It says on the leaflet that there will be a limited number of helicopter rides available for children, and to call if you want to know more. Perhaps Alice could put in a good word for Charlie and Annabel.'

Dan hadn't read that part of the leaflet; he'd been concentrating on Alice's message on the back, which he'd read more than once.

'Uh… I suppose that might be an idea.' It occurred to Dan that the only thing worse than calling Alice himself would be to stand listening to John speak with her. 'Shall I…'

'Go and get me another cup of coffee?' John asked. 'Yes, please do. And take your time. I'll be wanting to find out how Alice is doing in her new job.'

Two weeks later they were on the road, on a route that Dan had never expected to take. Back to Alice. Charlie and Annabel were in their car seats behind him, chattering excitedly, and John was beside him, suggesting traffic-free routes through London, which would be much more interesting for the kids than the view from the motorway.

The airfield was large and well organised, with people greeting everyone at the entrance and giving out fact sheets and activity packs for the kids. Entrance was free but there were tactfully placed collection boxes where people could give whatever they could afford. John and Dan both elbowed each other out of the way, and in the end both of them added their contribution to the fundraising venture, before following the stewards' instructions to start their tour in the control centre.

'Dad! Look!' Charlie's eyes were shining as they were ushered into the control room in small groups. Men and women were sitting at screens, and a woman turned, beckoning to the children.

'Would you like to come and see how we track our helicopters?'

Charlie caught his breath in delight, and John ushered him and Annabel across, peering over their heads as the woman explained what was on the screen in front of her. Dan hung back, allowing himself to soak in the impressive air of the operation.

Next, they were ushered through a ready room which their guide explained was currently empty, since all of the crews were currently outside. There was an area set aside for people to watch the helicopters take off and land, and Charlie was practically dancing with excitement as they walked out of the building and climbed the steps to the temporary viewing area.

Dan collected four pairs of folding binoculars, branded with the air ambulance logo, offering another donation to a smiling woman in exchange.

'Thanks. We'll be using this wisely. Enjoy your day.'

Enjoy wasn't really the word. Dan was moving in response to a compulsion which had an agenda all of its own. He handed three of the pairs of cardboard binoculars over to John and opened one himself, finding the lenses surprisingly good as he scanned the ground around the helicopters.

Alice. She was standing by the fuselage of one of the air ambulances, clad in the red uniform of the service and talking to an older man, who was holding a flight helmet. She seemed at ease. Happy even, her blonde curls shining in the sun. She looked around as another woman joined them, handing out cans of soft drinks and opening her own. Dan could almost see the shards of gold glinting in Alice's eyes.

This. This was what had taken her from him. Dan dismissed the thought. It had been her own yearning for a team, people she could trust to stick with her through thick and thin. His fear, and the compelling need to protect himself and Charlie from loss. The helicopters were just an eye-catching accessory after the fact.

He couldn't take his eyes off her. Staring at her through binoculars seemed intrusive and he reminded himself that this was an open day and the crews knew full well they were being watched. A sudden longing—the need to touch Alice and smell the scent of her hair—assailed him.

'Dad! I can see Alice!' Charlie started to shout and wave. 'Alice!'

'We're too far away, Charlie, she can't hear us.' He saw her bend and take something from the pocket in the leg of her jumpsuit, and heard John's voice behind him.

'Alice? We're on the viewing stand. We can see you.'

Charlie and Annabel started to jump up and down, waving, and John raised his free hand to signal his presence.

'Yes. Yes, right you are.' John ended the call. 'Alice says we can go down; they'll be ready for the trip we have booked shortly.'

Dan picked up Charlie's information pack from where he'd dropped it and stowed it under his arm along with Annabel's. John led the way, taking both children firmly by the hand and leading them across to the helicopter.

Charlie was tugging at John's hand and he let him run the last few metres into Alice's arms. Then Annabel got a hug, and Alice turned, introducing them to her team.

'This is Toby, he's the pilot, and Corinne, the co-pilot. Adam's our paramedic—he and I keep our patients safe for their trip to the hospital. Guys, these are my good friends, Charlie and Annabel.'

Dan hung back, watching her, his throat dry and his hands shaking. It was love at first sight all over again.

'Hi there.' Toby squatted down on his heels, solemnly shaking both Charlie and Annabel's hands. 'We won't be taking off for a little while, but perhaps you'd like to join me in the cockpit while we wait for everyone else.'

'Yes, please, yes, please!' Charlie seemed dumbstruck and Annabel answered for them both. Toby chuckled, climbing up into the cockpit and waiting while Alice lifted both of the children up to him.

'Don't touch anything…' John called over to the kids, and Alice grinned at him.

'That's okay, John, Toby has three of his own. He'll make sure they can't fly off without us.'

And then, suddenly they were alone. John had introduced himself to Corinne and Adam, plying them both with questions. Toby had pulled the door of the cockpit closed and there was only Alice. There only ever *could* be Alice.

'Thank you for coming.' A blush began to show on her cheeks. She felt something.

'Thanks for asking. And for the postcards. Charlie loves them.'

She nodded. 'Just because we don't see each other any more…'

'I know. I really appreciate it, Alice.'

'I was really happy to get one back from him. Thank you.'

They stared at one another. Dan desperately tried to think of something to say.

'I wasn't sure whether I'd see you today.'

'Where else would I be?' She turned the corners of her mouth down. 'I'm back on active service now.'

She didn't need to apologise for that. They were Dan's fears, not hers, and he was beginning to feel foolish. This place was so well organised, so quietly professional.

'And you're happy now that you're back?' The one and only thing that could make Dan feel better about anything right now was if Alice was happy.

'It's what I want, yes. And you?'

'John's been great, the practice is back running like clockwork and Charlie's doing really well at school. He still wants to be an air ambulance doctor, but he may change his mind and opt for pilot now.' Dan couldn't tell her that he was happy. 'It's…what I want.'

'Dan, I…' Alice reached forward as if she were about to touch him. The golden shards in her eyes made Dan catch his breath. Then she looked around as a man tapped her on the shoulder.

'Sorry to interrupt. Is this the helicopter that'll be going up next?' He indicated a woman with three children standing behind him.

'Yes. In five minutes, if you'd like to stand over there…' Alice indicated a spot by the fuselage and then turned her gaze back onto Dan. 'I've got to go; we'll be taking off shortly. May I see you when we get back?'

There was an insistence about the question that almost knocked Dan off his feet. She had more to say and suddenly that was the only thing in the world that Dan wanted to hear.

'I'll find you before we leave.' Wherever she was. However long it took.

'Thank you.' Alice turned suddenly, walking over to the families who were starting to gather around the helicopter, a bright smile on her face.

CHAPTER SEVENTEEN

DAN HAD WAITED, almost forgetting to wave to the helicopter as it flew over their heads in the viewing stand. John was talking to the family standing next to them, which Dan counted as an act of mercy, since all he could think about was Alice. All he could feel was the bright hope that maybe they could change the odds that were stacked against them, from impossible to just improbable. It was a small chance but it shone brightly, like a guiding star.

The airfield was cleared and everyone stood back for another helicopter to take off and then he saw Alice's heading back to the airfield. When the rotor blades stilled, parents hurried forward to collect their children, and Dan saw Adam and Toby lifting the kids down from the helicopter. John left him behind, going to collect Charlie and Annabel, and he spotted Alice walking back to the stand with them.

Then he saw Alice take her phone from her

pocket, looking at the screen. The loudspeaker crackled into life, suddenly a tone sounding.

'Ladies and Gentlemen, we need you to clear the helipads, please. Everyone behind the barriers. The helicopters will be taking off shortly and this is not an exercise. Repeat, this is not an exercise.'

Alice was on the alert, waving everyone around her forward. 'Behind the barriers, please. As quickly as you can… No, this isn't a demonstration; this one's for real…'

She looked up suddenly, her gaze finding him. 'Dan… Dan, wait for me!'

'As long as it takes…' John and Charlie looked up as he shouted over their heads at the top of his voice. Alice nodded, turning to jog back towards the helicopter.

There were more announcements and all of the stewards were working hard now, keeping everyone back. A tone sounded through the loudspeakers and the voice asked again for the signal that the area was clear. Then the rotor blades of two helicopters started to turn.

Silence fell amongst the crowd, and Dan picked both Annabel and Charlie up so that they could see. The helicopters rose together into the blue sky as people waved silently, some blowing kisses, others clearly sending prayers. This was for real, and while the craft had been exciting and eye-catching before, they were now majestic.

In one heart-stopping moment, Dan knew. He felt…so many things, but fear wasn't one of them. Alice was with her team, and part of a well-organised machine. She'd gone to save lives, not to spend her own.

As the helicopters disappeared into the horizon, a hum of conversation started to run around the crowd. Then the loudspeaker tone sounded again.

'*Thank you everyone, for helping us to get our crews off the ground quickly. Please give yourselves a round of applause…*' The announcer paused as clapping and cheering sounded around the airfield. '*We still have plenty to show you—there's a recently decommissioned helicopter in the field to the right of the helipads and our stewards will be there to tell you all about it. And there's a bouncy castle, along with refreshments. Thank you again for being part of the work of the air ambulance service.*'

'Magnificent.' John was as close as he ever got to being speechless.

'Has Alice gone to save someone?' Charlie asked, and Dan nodded.

'Yes. Alice and Adam will look after them while Toby and Corinne fly the helicopter to the hospital.'

'Does it take long?' Annabel rested her head on Dan's shoulder, clearly wondering if they'd be waiting around.

John shook his head. 'We can go for a snack and you can play on the bouncy castle if you like. Then I'll take you both home. Charlie, you'll come to tea with us?'

'Okay. Will you come, Dad?'

'I have to wait for Alice to come back…' He shot a querying look at John.

'That's right, Charlie. You can sleep at my house if your father's going to be late home and maybe we'll watch a film before bedtime. What do you think?'

Charlie nodded enthusiastically. He knew that John had a collection of all the latest films for kids, some of which he hadn't seen yet. 'Yes, please, Uncle John.'

Dan put Charlie and Annabel down, feeling in his pocket for his car keys. 'Thanks, John. I owe you one.'

'Nonsense. It's my pleasure…'

It was several hours before the helicopter was back at the airfield, and Alice was tired. There had been a pile-up on the motorway and both air ambulance teams had worked hard, stabilising patients so they could be transported to the hospital. They'd had to wait for several to be cut from the wreckage of their vehicles, and although they were very poorly, everyone was expected to live.

As the helicopter approached the airfield, Alice felt her heartbeat quicken. Toby swung the craft around in a wide arc, flying straight over the viewing stand.

'He's still here.' He could see directly beneath them through the landing window at his feet.

'Just land, Toby. Before he decides he's under surveillance and makes a run for it.' Alice tried to conceal the smile that sprang to her lips.

Toby peeled away, landing smack in the centre of the helipad. 'What are you going to say, Alice?' he called to her as she tugged the door open.

'I don't know. You can interrogate me later...'

But as she walked towards the stand and saw Dan coming to meet her, she knew exactly what she was going to say. She'd let him go, but now she was going to fight for him. She beckoned him over to the deckchairs which stood outside the cafeteria.

'Dan, I...' She couldn't say this reclining in a deckchair and so she stood up, and Dan followed suit. 'When you left, I was hurting and wanted to draw a line between Mallory Cross and me, the way I did before. But I can't.'

Dan smiled. 'So you sent postcards. Were they just for Charlie?'

'Yes—and no. I didn't want him to think I'd left him and I would have sent them even if they hadn't been for you as well.' The invitation hadn't just been for Charlie either, and maybe Dan knew that, too.

He nodded. 'I waited for them. Every week.'

Alice took a breath. Dan didn't much like risk, but she was going to take one. The biggest of her life. 'I know you think we can't make it, but we can. These guys…' She gestured to the team, who were still standing by the helicopter. 'They're my best friends. But they'll still be my friends if we don't see each other every day. You're my team. You and Charlie. If the job at the surgery's still open, I'd like to apply for it.'

He shook his head. 'Sorry, you're not a good fit. Your place is with the air ambulance service, and I was wrong to worry for you. I've seen that today.'

Alice thought for a moment. 'Or we both compromise. I'll come back to Cambridgeshire and apply for a transfer to the air ambulance service there. Doctors with experience are always in demand, and I'll know exactly what to say at the interview…' Suddenly anything seemed possible. Everything…

'I love you, Alice.' Dan was a little braver than her, and he could say the words. 'There's no going back on that now.' He took her hands between his. 'So all I can do is make sure you never want to leave me.'

'Dan…' She reached up, putting her arms around his neck. When she kissed him and he kissed her back… It was everything she'd ever wanted. A team, a lover, a friend.

'We don't need to *live* in Mallory Cross—I can

commute in to the practice…' He smiled down at her.

'Step in the dark, Dan. I love you too, and it makes me brave.'

'All the same…?'

She laid her finger over his lips and he fell silent. 'No, Dan. Mallory Cross was my home, and it can be again. Charlie's school is there and we have good friends who mean a great deal more than anyone who might disapprove of me. I don't care if they do, because I'll have you and… Do *you* want me there?'

'Do you really need to ask?'

'I want you to say it.' Alice gasped as he fell to one knee. She heard a whoop from the other side of the airfield and flapped her hand in that direction. 'They're watching and I didn't mean…'

'I mean it, Alice. I'll say it in front of your team and the whole village and anyone else who cares to listen. I want to say it right now, to show you that I'm in this for keeps. I love you.'

'I love you too, Dan.' There was only him. The whole world could be gawping at them, but all she'd see was Dan.

'We don't need to make things work, because they already do. Will you marry me, Alice?'

'Yes. I'll marry you. Just as soon I can get you to the church.' She sank down onto his knee, feeling his arms curl around her. Dan kissed her and she clung to him as her world tipped and everything changed.

'Are you afraid any more, Dan?'

'Not any more. You?'

'No.'

He kissed her again, and she heard Toby hollering across to them. He was still standing by the helicopter, with Adam and Corinne. 'Did she say *yes*?'

Dan laughed, shouting back, 'She said *yes*. Even though I don't have a ring…'

Alice chuckled. When she was a teenager she'd dreamed of a romantic proposal, over candlelight and a good dinner. But this was better. Sitting on Dan's knee, wearing her overalls, with her team shouting across a field at them. It was real, and witnessed by people who mattered.

'You don't know what you're saying, Dan…' Toby was climbing back into the cockpit. 'Toby's got a knack for improvisation.'

Toby disappeared for a moment then pulled back the window and dropped something down to Corinne, who started to sprint across the field towards them. She put Toby's offering into Dan's hand.

'Congrats, you two! From all of us.' Corinne turned, jogging away from them.

'What's this?' Dan opened his hand, looking at the slim circle of copper in his palm. 'Something to do with the helicopter?'

'That's state-of-the art equipment—I very much doubt it. It's probably one of Toby's things he's saved for later and never uses. Do you think it'll fit?'

Dan grinned. 'There's only one way to find out.'

She held out her finger and Dan slipped the makeshift ring carefully onto her finger. It fitted perfectly. 'It's gorgeous, Dan. Thank you.'

'I'll get you a proper one tomorrow.'

She didn't need diamonds. Alice got to her feet, waving over to Toby and the others, who waved back, picking up their gear and heading towards the hangar.

'Now that we're alone, shall we go home?' Alice caressed his cheek.

Dan nodded. 'Your place or mine? Although John's taken my car…'

'Mine's in the car park. Let's go to *our* home. Mallory Cross.'

EPILOGUE

ALICE HAD PLANS. Dan had plans. All of them were *their* plans.

She'd left the south-east air ambulance team, who had made their intentions for the future clear at a riotous party that Dan had organised. Alice had been reliably informed that she might run and she could even take up a job for four days a week with their Cambridgeshire counterparts. But she couldn't hide from their friendship.

It was an exciting time for the practice and Alice had decided to work there for the remaining one day a week to cement her ties with the community. John was staying on for the next year to see patients and help expand their services.

The home that she'd grown up in, which Alice had reluctantly decided to sell, was taken off the market. The sale of Dan's house provided them with the cash to seamlessly blend the old with the new, and the architect's drawings of a roomy extension at the back of the house had been approved. Alice was already choosing colours for their home.

The happiest of Christmases had come and gone, and all the dreams of a bright New Year had been toasted. It was time to turn their minds to the wedding.

At the end of January, and on the coldest day of winter so far, Alice was watching from the window as Dan's car drew up outside. She ran to the front door, flinging it open.

'You've got it?'

'I've got it.' He grinned, stamping the snow from his boots. 'Wait…wait.' Alice was already slipping her hands into the pockets of his weatherproof jacket, looking for the package he'd brought home with him.

'I thought that Toby was going to have to find some string in his pocket for you to tie around my finger tomorrow.'

'I wasn't going to let that happen.' Dan produced the longed-for parcel from a zipped pocket inside his jacket. 'You can look, but don't touch.' He took the ring from its box, holding it up.

Rose gold, its deep reddish hue giving more than a hint of copper. Alice caught her breath. 'It's beautiful, Dan. Much better than I thought it would be. Can't I just try it on?'

'No, it's the right size. The first time I put the old ring on your finger was the day we were engaged. The first time for this new ring is the day we're married.'

Dan had given her a diamond eternity ring to celebrate their engagement, but Alice hadn't been able to give up her plain copper ring and worn it next to its more costly counterpart. The dilemma of choosing a wedding ring had been solved when Dan had found a goldsmith who would combine copper and gold from scratch. Three weeks ago, they'd driven to Cambridge and Alice had handed over her treasured copper ring so that they could watch as it was melted down and combined with gold to make a small ingot of rose gold, ready to be tooled and polished to make a wedding ring.

'So we have everything we need now.' A dress, two rings and a village church were all that was required, along with Charlie to act as best man, under John McIntyre's supervision. They'd invited friends and family, organised a reception at the village hall and they were ready. Alice had modified the village tradition of a bride walking to the church with her father, and would walk to the church with Dan's parents, plus anyone else who tagged along as they made their way up the village high street.

'Yes. I may take Charlie over to John's place a little early. It's snowing already, and I don't want to have to spend the night here with you.'

'Would that be so bad?' Alice led him into the

sitting room to warm up in front of the fire that was blazing in the grate.

'We made our own rules for this wedding, and the least we can do is stick to them.' Dan sat down, curling his arm around her shoulder. 'If you do get snowed in, I'll be round in the morning to dig you out.'

'Come early. We can't get married with wet feet.' Alice kissed him. She'd marry Dan in a howling gale and knee deep in water if she had to. That wasn't her first choice, though.

'Don't worry. It'll take more than a bit of snow to stop us...'

Alice woke the next morning to the sound of metal scraping against paving stones. When she hurried downstairs, Norah was standing by the front door, barring her path.

'No, you don't. Dan's out there clearing the snow.'

'On his own? I'll go and put some clothes on and help him.'

'No, you won't. He has Toby and Adam with him, and half a dozen men from the village. Your job is to get into your dress, and we'll do your hair so that you're ready for ten o'clock. It might even be quicker to walk—the snowploughs probably aren't out yet and the roads look pretty treacherous.'

'That'll be okay, a lot of the farmers around

here have snowploughs and they usually take care of the village as well as their own land. If the worst comes to the worst, we can always hitch a ride on a tractor.'

'Well, if you think so…' Norah smiled suddenly. 'I'm sure we'll make it; they're doing a fine job with the drive. Come and have some breakfast and we'll get you ready…'

At ten o'clock sharp, Alice slipped on her sheepskin boots and Ted helped her into a warm woollen coat, carefully chosen to cover the hem of her dress without trailing on the ground during her walk to the church. Norah put the finishing touches to her hair and Alice pulled on her gloves before picking up her bouquet. Then Ted offered her his arm.

'Thank you.' Alice slipped her hand into the crook of his elbow.

'It's my privilege to stand in for your father.' Ted smiled at her, opening the front door.

The snow had been cleared for her, all the way down the front path. And at the end Dan stood, his hands stuffed in the pockets of the heavy coat he wore over his suit, his trousers tucked into a pair of sturdy hiking boots. Toby and Adam stood on one side of him, with John McIntyre and Charlie on the other. Geeta and Molly's husbands were there, too.

'Looks as if Dan's decided to amend the plan...' Ted murmured and Alice nodded, giving Dan a wave.

She walked to the end of the path on Ted's arm. The lane leading down to the high street was already ploughed and she could see a tractor up ahead of them, bedecked in white ribbons and mud from the road.

'I can't let you walk on your own in this weather.' Dan grinned. 'And since you have your coat on, there's no danger of my seeing your dress. May I sweep you off your feet?'

Norah was negotiating the ridge of snow in between the pavement and the road, waving away Toby's outstretched hand, and Alice was sure that she could manage it. But this was her wedding day. She laid her hand on his shoulder. 'Of course you may.'

The wedding party followed the tractor down to the high street and into the ploughed pathway along the middle of the road. As they passed the Swan Inn, air ambulance teams from Sussex and Cambridgeshire spilled out of the doors, along with partners and children. Toby's eldest daughter was wrapped up in a warm coat over her bridesmaid's dress, and John's granddaughter Annabel joined the procession with her mother. The two little girls found each other and walked hand in hand behind Alice, both excited to be bridesmaids for the first time.

Front doors opened and closed and the procession grew, laughing and joking in the crisp air. Dan felt in his pocket, passing Alice a handkerchief, and she dabbed at her eyes, trying not to ruin her make-up.

The path up to the church porch had been cleared and two snowmen stood by the entrance, one sporting a top hat and tie, and the other a white veil. Alice forgot all about her make-up as she started to cry happy tears, holding tight onto Dan's arm.

'I'll meet you at the altar. Don't make me wait too long…' Dan barely had time to whisper the words as they entered the large porch, decorated with flowers and winter foliage, before Norah hurried her up the stone steps to the room above the porch, where several comfortable chairs and a full-length mirror awaited them.

She was too excited to think about anything, or anyone, other than Dan. Finally, Norah was satisfied that she and her two young bridesmaids were looking their best and allowed them back down the stairs, where Ted was waiting to accompany Alice on the best journey of her life.

The porch was full of coats and boots and there was standing room only in the church, even though the vicar had brought in extra chairs from the church hall. Dan waved to Molly and Geeta and their families and also spotted Jasmine and her parents, and Elaine and her husband and children. It seemed that the whole village had turned out to wish them well on their wedding day.

He took his place next to Charlie and John, who were wearing matching green waistcoats under their jackets. Charlie leaned across, climbing onto his knee.

'Don't worry, Dad. Everything will go fine.' John had clearly been schooling Charlie in his responsibilities as best man, and reassuring the groom must have come at the top of the list.

'Thanks, Charlie. I'm feeling good.'

Charlie nodded sagely. 'Me too.' He turned to John. 'Have you got the rings, Uncle John?'

That had to be the fiftieth time he'd asked this morning, but John smiled, patting the pocket on his green embroidered waistcoat. 'Right here, Charlie. We don't need them just yet.'

The chatter in the church quieted suddenly as the first chords of the wedding march sounded. Dan turned, and as Alice entered the church on his father's arm he sprang to his feet.

She looked so beautiful. So happy. Alice was wearing a dress with a lace bodice and an A-line skirt, the hemline swirling three inches above her ankles. High-heeled shoes completed the look, and she'd added a touch of the countryside with a bouquet of winter foliage, gypsophila and trailing eucalyptus. Her blonde hair curled around a delicate floral crown, and as she neared him he saw the golden shards in her eyes blaze.

'You take my breath away.' Dan took her hand when she reached him.

'It's been a long journey...' She smiled up at him. 'But every step was worth it, because it brought me here, to you.'

This moment was theirs alone. And yet... Dan grinned at her. 'I guess it *does* take a village to make a wedding.'

* * * * *